Blue Christmas

Blue Christmas

Paul McCusker

Augustine Institute
Greenwood Village, CO

Augustine Institute
6160 S. Syracuse Way, Suite 310
Greenwood Village, CO 80111
Tel: (866) 767-3155
www.augustineinstitute.org

Cover Design: Lisa Marie Patterson

This is an extensively rewritten version of the novel *Epiphany*,
originally published by the author, Paul McCusker, in 1999.

ISBN: 978-1-7325247-7-4
Library of Congress Control Number 2018954561

Printed in Canada ♾

To Dan Miller, for all those
Christmases so long ago.

Chapter One

LIKE MOST people, I never thought very much about death. Even as a late-to-the-party Catholic, with all of its emphasis on mortality and the after-life, death remained a distant point in time, a far shore on the horizon, the thing that happened to other people. The death of my wife Kathryn five years ago, from a brain tumor that had taken her quickly, still left me ambivalent about death. Her circumstances were exceptional, I told myself. Like being hit by a bolt of lightning. I expected to live for a very long time and then shuffle off my mortal coil.

So you can imagine my disappointment when I died at the relatively young age of sixty-two.

It was a stupid accident that killed me; one I'm a little embarrassed to confess. I had walked to the pond behind my house—not directly behind the house, but down the path through the grove of pine trees, just across the stone bridge and another dozen yards beyond that.

For years I loved walking around that pond first thing in the morning, sometimes in the afternoons. Copper, my Labrador, demanded it up right until the day he died. We walked to enjoy the pebbled shore, the soft earth and balding patches of grass and weeds, the gentle ripples of water. Sometimes Kathryn joined me. Not often, though. Arthritis in her knees took care of that. So Copper and I went, never knowing what we'd find there. New ducklings, a species of bug we'd never noticed before, fallen leaves of beautiful color and design, a subtle change in the shape of the pond after a particularly bad rain. The wonder of it all.

Even after I lost Copper I continued my excursion to the pond, though it changed after a developer had bought up Cahill's property to the west and cardboard boxes that pretended to be houses were quickly assembled. They called the development *Quail Run*; though I've never seen quail in the area. With the houses, of course, came more and more people. I didn't mind that. I like people. But some of those people had teenagers who'd decided that my pond was a good place to socialize. I don't mind teenagers wanting a place to socialize, but they had a lack of respect for the pond that annoyed me. Soda cans, food wrappers, and cigarette butts threatened to destroy the natural wonder of my haven.

So, it was this morning—if it *was* this morning, I can't be sure right now—I had walked down to the pond after pulling boxes of Christmas ornaments down from the attic. I'd bought a tree from Billy Atkinson's farm yesterday, and he and I had lugged it into my living room. My plan was to get everything set up for Christmas, then maybe grab the mail and go down to the Park 'N Dine for the breakfast special. That combination was a weakness of mine. The mail, the Park 'N Dine, and their blue-plate specials. There was magic in all three. The mail because it had letters, magazines, or even the odd manuscript from someone who didn't know I'd retired from my little publishing business. The Park 'N Dine because it was an old fifties-style diner with red cushions and chrome railings and beveled mirrors behind the pie rack and classic rock-and-roll on the Wurlitzer jukebox. The breakfast special because there was a lot of food for not a lot of money.

But I had to have my walk to the pond first. It was a bright December day. The kind of day where the air tingled against my cheeks and was so fresh it felt cleansing to breathe it in. The iced puddles on the hard earth cracked beneath my rubber-soled boots as I walked. It had snowed last night, so I was pretty sure the teenagers had stayed home and left my pond alone. It would be mine again, I was certain.

And it was.

The snow gave way to a deep freeze before dawn. The pond and the surrounding trees wore a magical coat of sparkling icicles. White frost clung to the branches like pairs of new gloves. The pond had a glaze of sugared ice. I took my seat on the large rock—*my* spot for years—and thought of Copper first, imagining I could hear him running around, sniffing and barking at unseen guests.

For a moment I thought of Kathryn as a younger woman, gesturing happily at a new discovery she'd made on the edge of the water. I thought of our children as their younger selves, long before their ambitions took them away. I thought of the winter when the pond had frozen over and my three kids skating and laughing, their cheeks bright red, their eyes wide and wet. The sharp wind could not stop their grace.

But then the memory vanished as my eye caught a french-fries container half-stuck in the ice, just along a particularly marshy area. I grumbled at whoever had left it there and climbed off my rock to retrieve the offending litter. I had taken only two steps when I felt an itch just under my shirt, something on my chest. It was just a dull itch as if a bug had made its way through my three layers of clothes to give me a bite. I reached up to scratch. That's when I slipped on the uneven stone.

I don't remember clearly what happened next, but I think my head hit something hard.

I felt so foolish that I laughed out loud.

I struggled to my feet and began to dust myself off, only to realize that I wasn't on my feet at all. I was still prone, half on the shore, half on the fractured ice, my eyes staring upwards at the December sky.

You may have a few questions at this point. So do I. Dying didn't give me instant knowledge about the secrets of the universe. Not the way I'd hoped it would. I'm a little disappointed about that.

Right now—whatever now is—I can only guess that time and space seem meaningless. That's why I can say I died this morning without knowing if it was really this morning or last week or last year or eons ago. For all I know, everything I'm experiencing and seeing now may be like the fading light from a distant star.

This is terribly befuddling for a man of mixed religious pedigree like myself. As a Baptist who'd once made a heartfelt profession of faith at the age of eleven after a week-long revival, I thought I would go to Heaven the instant I had died. Years later, when I became an Episcopalian to suit Kathryn, I assumed I would have a pit-stop on the way to Heaven, just to clear up any misunderstandings about my life and what I believed. Later still, after Kathryn and I both became Catholic, I accepted that I didn't know what exactly would happen to me after death. Purgatory, maybe? I don't know. I don't seem to be in Heaven or Hell or anywhere my theology can put its finger on. I'm simply here *and not* there.

For a moment here *was near the pond. Then, without knowing how it happened,* here *was an apartment belonging to my son Jonathan. How I knew it was his apartment is a puzzle to me. I had never seen his apartment when I was alive. He lived somewhere near Phoenix.*

Now I knew why he'd never invited me to visit. His apartment was a depressing single-room studio with a tiny refrigerator and stove, card-table and folding chair, a bed, and a dresser. A roach skittered across the floor. The wallpaper was water-stained and peeling. The carpet, which was worn through to the bare floor in patches, smelled of mildew. It was upsetting to see where he lived.

A small alarm clock next to the bed said it was seven minutes past five. I had been dead for eight hours—*if* I had died in the morning and this was later that same day. The sun was gone, though I wondered if the sun's rays ever reached this tenement, nestled as it was between two larger apartment buildings.

I heard a key slip into the lock on the door. A moment later, Jonathan Lee, my second son, walked in. I braced myself. How was I going to explain how—or why—I was there?

He looked past me and around the apartment with a weary expression, as if the sight of the apartment was as offensive to him as it was to me. He was bundled in a winter coat his mother had given to him right before she died. It looked the worse for wear. He carried a hard hat and his jeans were covered in dry-wall dust. His face, a masculine version of Kathryn's, was lean and stubbled. He looked older than his twenty-eight years, tired and sad. That bothered me. He tossed the hard hat on the card table. His brown hair was cropped surprisingly short. He'd had a ponytail last time I saw him. When was that? Last fall when he came to visit.

He dropped by on his way to Wyoming. Some kind of business opportunity that later didn't pan out.

He dropped his coat on the bed and crossed over to the sink. He began to make coffee. He stared for a moment out the small window over the sink. It afforded a view of a brick wall, probably an alley below. While the coffee brewed, he wandered over to the far wall beyond the bed. An easel I hadn't noticed stood in the corner. He lifted the tarp covering the easel. I caught a glimpse of a sketch but couldn't make out the details.

I felt relieved. At least he was still drawing, if not actually painting. He was a gifted artist. I was glad to see that he was still at work.

Or was he?

He dropped the tarp and turned away with a look of disgust.

My heart ached for him. Something had changed in him over the past couple of years. He withdrew from me—and his art. *Why?* I asked him to the point of nagging. On one occasion he answered—more of a dismissive mumble than an answer—and said he was suffering from "artist's block." That was all he said, and we spoke no more on the subject.

A cell phone rang on the table. Jonathan stared at it as if he might not bother to pick it up. I hoped he would.

It was Father Cliff Montgomery from my parish church of St. Clare of Assisi. How I knew that so certainly I can't really say. But I knew it was him. I knew it had something to do with me.

On the sixth ring, Jonathan snatched up the phone. "Hello?" he said.

Father Cliff offered cursory greetings and then told him that I was dead with that sweet, gentle voice Father Cliff used when it came to bad news.

Jonathan looked stunned and slowly slid into the chair next to the table.

"I found him by the pond," Father Cliff explained. "We were supposed to have lunch together and when your father didn't show, I went to look for him."

I wondered why I didn't see Father Cliff find my body. Why had I been whisked away from seeing that moment reaction, from watching the ambulance come, from all the things that had happened between then and now?

I could imagine it, though. Poor Father Cliff arriving at the pond, the alarm he must have felt to see me lying there. He and I had become good friends over the past few years, and I was sure that my sudden departure shocked him, as his death would have shocked me.

And, good friend that he was, he'd taken it upon himself to track down my children to break the news.

Why had he decided to call Jonathan first? David was the oldest and, thinking about it, I assumed etiquette demanded that David be at the top of the list. Yet Father Cliff called Jonathan first, just as I'd thought of Jonathan first. Was there a connection? I could only guess that Father Cliff knew as I did that, though Jonathan had the sensitivities of an artist, he was actually the strongest of my three kids.

Or maybe it was the only phone number for my kids Father Cliff had.

Jonathan leaned onto the table and rubbed his mouth. "I'll call David and Ruth, then drive up right away." He put down the phone and stood up, pacing for a moment. Then he sat on the edge of his bed. He had a wild-eyed look, like his emotions were at war deep inside of him. Then he flung himself backward onto the mattress, covering his eyes with his arms. He was still. His breathing was steady. I couldn't even tell whether or not he was crying.

But I *felt* his grief and had *impressions* of his thoughts. A sense of loss, of emptiness, of confusion.

Then I was away again.

David was in a hotel room in New York. A large and spacious suite that looked larger than my house. He was on the phone, pacing, talking in that way he did when he was negotiating. He was playing hardball with someone on the other end, threatening about what would happen if they didn't act *now* while the stocks were at a good price.

The phone buzzed in his hand. He looked at the screen. He made a few more points to the poor person on the other end. I felt badly that Jonathan's news would interrupt David's business call. I could tell by the way his lips were thin and tight that he was about to secure the deal. His lips always did that when we played Monopoly as a family and he was about to foreclose.

He looked at the screen and then pushed the button.

"This is a surprise," David said to Jonathan as he shoved some papers into his briefcase and pocketed a gold pen into his suit-jacket.

He turned and went into the bathroom, grabbing at his toiletries and pushing them into a leather shaving kit. He listened to Jonathan for a moment and then lowered the toilet cover and sat down. I couldn't hear Jonathan as clearly as I heard Father Cliff.

David asked a few questions to make sure he had the details right—found by the pond, dead—and then he looked at his watch.

He would grab the next flight from LaGuardia to Denver. He pushed another button and dropped the phone onto the counter. He stood up and pressed his hands onto the edge of the sink, lowering his head. He took a deep breath, then looked at himself in the bathroom mirror. His round face was uncannily like Kathryn's brother Stan, except with my eyes. He looked a sickly pale. He lifted the toilet cover as if he might vomit. Then he took another deep breath, straightened up, and, with a final look at the mirror, ran his fingers through his perfectly cut black hair.

His phone buzzed again. He picked it up and looked at the screen. His hands trembled.

I was aware then of how different David was from Jonathan. They were opposites, I could say. David puts on a very convincing strong-man act, but inside he's soft and vulnerable. He clutched the phone and slumped down onto the floor, his back to the tiled wall next to the shower.

A knock on the bathroom door. A woman's voice asked, "David? Are you all right?"

"Yeah," he said, his voice raspy. "Get me a cab. And tell the office I'm not coming back today."

Whoever it was on the other side of the door padded away.

David yanked a wash cloth from the rail and shoved it into his mouth to stifle any noise he might make as he wept.

I wanted to comfort him. I tried to touch his heaving shoulders and couldn't.

The glow of the bathroom light in David's hotel room suddenly dimmed, and I was in a cozy darkness—like the darkness of a small closet.

Did I will myself there? No. But there I was nonetheless.

I was sitting in a chair. Outside I heard traffic. Whatever light came from behind the large curtained window was manmade. It was night, though I didn't know if it was night on the same day or on some other day.

The silhouettes of a couch, a coffee table, and a stand with a lamp were outlined by a light that hung just above a door. It took a moment for me to realize that I was in my daughter's apartment in one of the sections of Los Angeles. I knew only because I had seen it from her computer camera when she'd called me using one of those video services. She had given me a tour after she'd moved in, so I would know she was doing all right in the big city.

She wasn't, and I knew it. She'd gone there to be an actress—like so many other young girls—and wound up working at a coffee shop while trying to get auditions. She also waitressed at a nearby cocktail lounge. The apartment was small and dingy—an efficiency, of sorts. I was in what might have been the living room. There was a counter with over-hanging cupboards separating a small kitchen beyond it. A door to the left led to a tiny bedroom and bathroom.

I heard voices on the other side of the door, loud and laughing, and then the door itself flew opened and a small crowd of people swarmed in. A young man they called Jeffrey fumbled for the light switch and nearly knocked a picture off of the wall.

"Be careful," Ruth said as she closed the door behind her.

The dozen young people—all in their early twenties like her—looked like they'd just come from a party. I immediately sensed their comradery. They were a group that did a lot of things together. But I had an immediate feeling that Ruth didn't like them very much. Her expression, the way she looked at them, made me think they were there, not out of affection or enjoyment of their company, but out of necessity.

I sensed they all felt the same way about each other. They were like survivors in a lifeboat.

I stood up and moved to a corner behind the chair. I bumped a small Christmas tree Ruth had set up. The cheap plastic balls shook and the little bells jingled.

If I were some kind of spirit, I wondered how I had bumped into the tree.

Ruth looked in my direction, her brow furrowing.

The crowd pressed into the apartment and made themselves at home, chatting happily, and guffawing at jokes I didn't understand. One attractive girl with deep dimples giggled, stumbled, and fell into the lap of a young man.

Ruth moved to the small kitchen. She held up two bottles of wine, already opened and half-finished. "Help yourself," she said and put them next to a stack of paper cups.

One young man leapt at the offer.

Turning to the opposite counter, Ruth called over her shoulder, "I'm making coffee. Anybody want some?"

A dark-haired boy with a loose tie and obvious lust for the girl with the dimples complained: "I want something stronger."

"This is all I have," my daughter replied in the flat, no-nonsense tone of voice she'd inherited from her mother. Her friends were oblivious to her, her tone, and her coffee. They carried on with their reveling, probably begun at some other Christmas party. One couple—a blonde-haired boy and rather heavy-set girl—fell onto the couch and whispered conspiratorially about sneaking into the bedroom together. Someone turned on music. An aggressive voice shouted what sounded like "I'll Be Home for Christmas."

A boy in an oddly festive suitcoat of red and green came to my spot in the corner. I moved out of his way, crossing in front of a large curtained window to another corner with a large plastic version of a houseplant. It had a coating of dust on it. My daughter hadn't inherited her mother's house-cleaning skills.

Ruth drifted around the counter and went to the large window next to me. She pushed the curtains aside and stared sadly at the Los Angeles skyline, a montage of steel with lights of whites and reds and greens. She sighed and folded her arms.

I'm tempted to say that she was beautiful, like my wife Kathryn. That would be wrong. She was *more* beautiful than Kathryn was. Somehow, she'd been blessed with the best features from both our sides of the family. Large hazel eyes set upon perfectly rounded cheeks, a dainty nose and full lips, and brown hair that fell magically into place no matter how many times she ran her fingers through it. She was tall and shapely, but with a build that drew men's glances no matter where she was or what she wore. My daughter, I may say as objectively as possible, was worthy of a poet's raptures or a painter's eye.

A boy with close-cut dark hair and a weird jewel in the middle of his ear came up behind her. "What's so interesting?" he asked as he wrapped his arms around her waist. He kissed her on the neck.

My heart sunk as I knew—in this strange way that I could know anything—that my daughter had shared her bed with this boy, not out of love but loneliness, and even now she regretted it. He was the kind of kid who feigned affection, not as a lover but as a conqueror. He'd had her once, he wanted her again, just for the bragging rights. She realized too late what kind of person he was.

She slipped from the boy's grasp—his name was Terry—and said "Coffee" as if that answered his question. She made her way back to the kitchen.

He smirked.

I had the rather coarse desire to slap the smirk off his face.

Ruth was pouring the coffee when her cell phone rang. Half the partiers reached for their pockets, thinking it was theirs.

Putting down the coffeepot, Ruth reached for the phone, her elbow brushing one of the mugs and knocking it over. "Get that, Terry?" she cried out as she quickly grabbed some paper towels to mop up the mess.

"Hey," Terry said into the phone. It was Jonathan, who asked for Ruth. "Who's this?"

Ruth disappeared behind the counter to clean the coffee on the floor.

Terry cupped his hand over the phone and said, "It's some guy named Jonathan."

Ruth reappeared, still clutching the soggy paper towel. "Jonathan?" She looked worried and took the phone from Terry. Leaning onto the counter, her left elbow touched the edge of a small puddle of spilled coffee that soaked into the fabric of her sweater. She didn't notice. "I'm sorry," she said to Jonathan. "My phone was off. I haven't looked at it. I didn't see any messages."

She turned her back to the partiers, her voice and emotions going with her. Her head dropped down. Then she slowly turned around again and put the phone down. Her eyes were red.

"What's wrong?" Terry asked. He rounded the counter to touch her, but she bristled, and he stepped back.

"Party's over," she said sharply. "Everyone has to go. *Now.*"

"What? Why?" Terry asked. He was clearly surprised, not because she wanted everyone to leave, but that she sounded so harsh.

"Out!" she cried. "My father is dead." She rushed into her bedroom.

The partiers went quiet. Terry shrugged at them. It was an indication of this crowd's level of friendship that no one offered to stay to help or console her.

Terry had the nerve to pout. His hope of sleeping with my daughter later that night had been foiled. That alone made me think my death was worthwhile.

They all herded out like the cattle they were.

Alone my daughter wept uncontrollably on the edge of her bed. I saw her. I reached out to her. But, as had happened with David, I could not penetrate the barrier of time and space, flesh and spirit. Apparently, I could bump a small Christmas tree and make it move, but I couldn't offer comfort to my own daughter.

Chapter Two

I'M AWARE *of time. Not of its passing, but its absence. It's a strange adjustment. I now have to concentrate very hard on the markers, the means by which I once measured the passing of time. I'm not talking about watching the hands move on a clock, or a digital number kick over, I mean the activities that move time forward: the time it took Ruth to figure out plane tickets, pack, walk to her car, and drive on the tangled web of freeways to get to an airport.*

I don't know how long it really took for her to land in Denver, rent a car, and drive to her hometown and my home in Hope Springs. It felt like mere seconds to me, if "seconds" is a word I can use. If this were a movie, someone might call it a "dissolve," where we moved from the scene in her apartment to her standing next to my undecorated Christmas tree in my living room.

But even a "dissolve" indicates a passing of time. Now the words fail me. I know only that eternity is not time without end, but existence without time. It simply isn't here to count or measure. Were I not witnessing my loved ones who were trapped in *time, I would not even think about it.*

Ruth also thought about time as she stood in the center of my living room. Only, for her, the feeling was that time had stopped. The

Sears replica Victorian-style couch and matching love seat, the plush easy-chair, the gold lamps, end-tables, imitation classic-paintings and photos on the walls and mantle above the small brick fireplace—these were unchanged for as long as Ruth could remember.

Kathryn and I were not conscious of fashion or trends. We bought furniture that we liked and hoped would endure. We decorated our home modestly, from both our sense of taste and our budgetary constraints. If nothing else, we were consistent. On the rare occasions when any of the kids came to visit, they came to a familiar place. We thought they needed at least one constant in their tumultuous lives: the home where they grew up.

After Kathryn died, I got all kinds of suggestions from family and friends about the house. Some thought I should move. Some said I should re-arrange things, get new furniture, make adjustments, all to keep from being reminded of her in my grief. I felt the opposite. I wanted to keep everything just as it was so I would be reminded of her when my grief subsided.

"Oh, Daddy," Ruth said sadly. She hugged her overcoat close. Her eye caught my compact disc of Elvis's Christmas album sitting on the end table. I had played it while bringing the boxes of Christmas decorations down from the attic that morning. "Blue Christmas," she said.

My eye went to the clock on the mantle. It was seventeen minutes past two in the morning.

The subdued roar of a car drew my attention to the front window. Jonathan's Volkswagen van, I knew.

It was light outside. The sun was up.

Confused, I looked at the clock on the mantle again. It was ten minutes to nine. Ruth was sound asleep on the sofa, her coat draped over her like a blanket.

Jonathan cut off the engine. A door slammed.

Ruth stirred, then sat up. She heard footsteps on the porch. She leapt to her feet and, like her younger self, skipped to the door and pulled it open just as Jonathan reached for the handle.

"Hiya," he said. He parked a large suitcase against the wall and gave her a long hug.

Snow swirled around them. The lawn and driveway were covered with an inch of it.

Ruth buried her face in his shoulder and sobbed.

"You'll freeze your tears if we stay out here," he said, then retrieved his suitcase and guided her into the house. He closed the door.

"I can't believe it." Her voice quivered. "I talked to him a week ago. He was fine. And then . . . I just can't believe it."

"I know," Jonathan said and handed her a tissue.

She dabbed at her eyes, careful not to smear what was left of her make-up. "He didn't say anything about heart problems. Dr. Mason said he was strong as a bull at his last check-up. How can you have a heart attack when you're strong as a bull?"

A heart attack? I'd died of a heart attack? Is that what the tickle in my chest was?

I felt a wave of relief. A fatal heart attack I could cope with. Killing myself by slipping on a rock was embarrassing.

Ruth continued, "Dr. Mason thought it was because he carried the Christmas tree in with Billy Atkinson last night. Then he brought all the boxes down from the attic."

"He got the boxes by himself?" Jonathan asked.

"By himself."

When did she get all this information? I wondered. Had she called Father Cliff when I couldn't see her? As with my other questions, there was no answer. What I saw—and *didn't* see—was beyond my control.

"Somebody should've been here," Ruth said. Guilt welled up with her tears. Of the three, Ruth had the least to feel guilty about where I was concerned. She was the most conscientious about phone calls and visits.

Jonathan said gently, "Don't do this to yourself."

She nodded, not whole-heartedly taking his advice. "David left a note in the kitchen."

"He's here already? That was fast," Jonathan said. "It took me almost twelve hours to drive from Phoenix."

Ruth half-smiled. "David has means of flight that we mere mortals don't. He's meeting Father Cliff at the funeral home as soon as he gets in."

"Should we be there?" Jonathan asked.

"He said he'd call us." Ruth suddenly grabbed for her coat. "My phone! I'm always forgetting where I put it."

Jonathan rolled his eyes. "I know."

She retrieved her phone from her coat pocket and looked at the screen. "No messages."

Jonathan drifted to the Christmas tree, gently touching a gold and red ornament shaped like an icicle.

Ruth sat down on the couch, tucking her legs underneath her like Kathryn used to do. Blowing her nose, she stared vacantly for a moment, then asked: "How are things in Phoenix?"

He shrugged. "The same old stuff. I'm foreman now."

"What does that mean?"

"I get to wear a different color hard-hat than the rest of the guys. Sometimes I boss them around—when they let me. Is there any coffee?" He walked off to the kitchen before she could answer. By the sounds of the banging cupboard doors, he was trying to find the means to make some.

I stood in the dining room, in-between the living room and kitchen. I pointed to the cabinet where I kept the coffee. It didn't help.

Ruth was on her feet and zoomed past me to rescue him. At the counter, she nudged him aside and asked: "Any new paintings?" She tried to make it sound like a casual question.

Jonathan shook his head. "Not much time for that kind of thing. What about you? You're still one of those secretaries—"

"A temporary assistant," she corrected him. "When I'm not at the coffee shop or the Toluca Lounge."

She set up the coffee maker and began the routine to make a pot.

Silence fell between them. I had the sudden feeling that they knew very little about each other's lives. They were like acquaintances rather than family. Until this moment, I had thought—*hoped*—that they kept in touch with each other, if not with me.

"Do you like Los Angeles?"

Ruth leaned against the counter. "Not especially. But that's where you have to go for the kind of career I want."

"Acting?"

She shrugged. "I don't know anymore. I don't know what I want to do. These days it seems like I work hard just to pay the bills and have some fun. That's the extent of my life."

The coffee maker choked and gurgled.

"Hmm," Jonathan said thoughtfully. "That must be why you look so tired."

Ruth touched her face and eyes self-consciously. "Do I look tired?" She launched from the counter and went to the mirror hanging in the dining room. She massaged her eyes. "Oh no. I have to look happy and healthy and carefree."

Jonathan laughed.

Ruth was serious. "I can't have Jan Binnocek yapping to everyone about how Los Angeles is wearing me out. You know she will."

"Why should you care what Jan Binnocek—or *anybody*—says?" Jonathan growled.

"Because... well, *because*," Ruth replied as if the second "because" answered his question.

Jonathan merely gazed at her.

"You know how they were when I left," she said. "'Oh, there goes little Miss Prima Donna—off to the West Coast for fame and fortune.'" For this last quote, Ruth put her hands on her hips and did a reasonably good impression of Nancy Melville. Nancy was the busybody who worked at the Quick Stop grocery store on Gallatin Avenue.

Jonathan raised an eyebrow. "You were after fame and fortune? I had no idea."

"No! That isn't why I went."

"Oh," Jonathan said, then added with a wry grin. "That's why *I* went."

The coffee was ready. Ruth nabbed two mugs from the rack to the left of the refrigerator.

Jonathan looked chagrinned as she sat them on the counter. "These are new," he said as he lifted up both mugs. Each had an image of Elvis on them. One was a headshot of him as a young man from his "Hound-dog" era. The other mug had an image from his white-sequined-jumpsuit-in-Las Vegas period.

Jonathan poured the coffee, and I knew he would later claim the mugs as his own, given the chance.

Ruth was moping. "I wanted to get out of here. Is that so terrible?" she said. "Is it so wrong to try to make something of yourself outside of Hope Springs?"

She yanked open the refrigerator door to pull out some half-and-half. I tried to remember how fresh it was. When did I last go shopping?

Jonathan smiled patiently at her. "You're pleading your case to the wrong person. "I was the promising young artist who would make a name for himself in one of New York's great art exhibits. I made a name, all right. I went from canvas to dry wall in record time. And I never even made it to New York. David did."

Ruth sighed.

"Few things happen the way we want them to," Jonathan said with a dismissive wave of his hand. It was one of my gestures.

Jonathan and Ruth returned to the living room. Ruth sat down on the couch again and sipped her coffee while Jonathan slipped into my easy chair. They were silent and the scene looked cozy, apart from the underlying unfamiliarity between them. I remembered the two of them sitting like that when Kathryn died. Here they were again—on the occasion of my death.

That gave me pause. What will motivate them to meet up when they've run out of dead people to bring them together?

Two cars pulled up outside. Through the front I saw one I recognized: the vintage American Motors Rambler that belonged to Father Cliff Montgomery. The second car was an innocuous modern car that could have been anything. I suspected it was a rental car driven by David.

Jonathan and Ruth also heard the cars but didn't move. They watched the door to see if whoever it was would knock or simply walk in. There was footfall on the porch and the door opened, David leading the way, with Father Cliff trailing behind.

David looked perfectly groomed, assuredly pristine, in his black overcoat, pressed trousers and shiny shoes. The son I'd seen crying in a hotel bathroom was now composed and in control. There was business to be taken care of and nobody could do it like my David. Or so he wanted everyone to think

Father Cliff, on the other hand, looked bad. He was a youngish priest, but his slender face seemed to sag and there was an uncharacteristic stubble on his chin that gave him the look of a man having a terrible hangover. His blue eyes were red-rimmed. His normally perfect black hair was disheveled. He wore an old heavy coat that made his usual upright military-school posture look like he was slouching, as if my death hung on him like chains.

Father Cliff and Jonathan shook hands, and Ruth embraced him warmly. Ruth started to cry again, and I thought Father Cliff would join her. But he shook his head suddenly and said, "Plenty of time for that later."

David formally shook Jonathan's hand and received a quick hug from Ruth. It was awkward. On this I wasn't surprised. David never gave nor took affection very well. I suspect he thought of it as a sign of weakness. Weak people often do.

"I was wondering when you two would arrive," David said. "What time did you get here?"

"After midnight," Ruth replied.

"An hour ago," said Jonathan. "Not all of us have our own jets," he added.

"It's not mine," David said quickly. "I was lucky it was available."

Ruth and Jonathan shot each other amused looks.

"You look wonderful," Father Cliff said, waving a hand at her. "A little tired, perhaps, but wonderful."

Ruth smiled, but self-consciously touched her face and eyes again.

"This town hasn't been the same without you." His eyes swept passed the three of them. "All of you. We miss the Lee kids. I wish you'd come back. I know your father did."

Awkward shuffles and mumbles from my normally articulate brood.

"So—you were both at the funeral home?" Jonathan asked, an obvious change of subject.

Ruth looked at David anxiously. "Did you . . . see Dad?"

"Yes," David said without elaborating. He tugged at his leather gloves to get them off. "I think we've covered all the details."

"What details?" Ruth asked.

"The business arrangements."

Jonathan looked coolly at David. "Business."

"Yes, *business*. The McWilliams Funeral Home is a business like anything else." David hung his overcoat on the rack by the door.

Jonathan stiffened. "And I'm sure you negotiated soundly, squeezed out every penny, got to the bottom line, and struck the best deal on behalf of our father."

"Jonathan," Ruth said in a low, admonishing tone. She put a hand on his arm.

Jonathan shook his head.

Father Cliff said, "There was a lot that needed doing, Jonathan."

Jonathan turned away. "There's coffee, if anyone wants some."

"I'd love some," Father Cliff said. He and Jonathan walked off to the kitchen.

"Whether it's funerals, building houses, or selling cotton candy, business is business," David called after Jonathan. "Mr. McWilliams knows that, and so do I. You can't blame me for making sure we aren't taken advantage of."

"You make it sound like you were haggling over a new car," Jonathan shouted back.

"Never mind," Ruth whispered to David.

David shrugged and said loudly, "If you want to go back and make some other arrangements with Mr. McWilliams, then feel free."

"Please, David," Ruth said.

Jonathan returned from the kitchen with a mug of coffee. "Not me," he said. "You're the wheeler-dealer. If you say you got the best deal, then I wouldn't say otherwise."

"So, what's the problem?"

"Nothing."

"Good."

"Good."

"Coffee, David?" Father Cliff asked from the kitchen doorway.

"I'll get it," David said and strode out.

Father Cliff turned his attentions to Ruth once more. "Some of the parishioners have told me over and over how much they miss your piano playing at church. Oh, and Ted Hagan asked me to pass along his greetings and condolences."

"Little *Teddy* Bear?" Jonathan said. "I thought he moved after he got his degree."

"Not every young person in this town felt obliged to leave us," Father Cliff teased.

"Ted's very sweet," Ruth said with a non-committal politeness. "Thank him for me."

"You can thank him yourself. He hopes to see you while you're here if you have a chance. Maybe you could stop by his shop when you're out and about—if you think it's appropriate, all things considered."

Father Cliff never let incidentals like a death or a funeral get in the way of his matchmaking. He often said he thought Ruth and Ted should have gotten married.

David returned from the kitchen. "Ted has a shop? I thought he aspired to become the manager of the Park 'n' Dine?"

"It's a combination coffee and second-hand book shop," Father Cliff said to David, but kept his gaze on Ruth. "He's never stopped thinking about you, Ruth."

Ruth frowned. "He doesn't know me. I'm not the girl he dated in high school."

"Has Los Angeles changed you that much?" Father Cliff asked.

"Apart from looking tired?" Jonathan asked, smiling.

Ruth punched him.

"I'm just saying, if you have the time, stop by the shop."

"If I get a chance," Ruth said, then turned away from Father Cliff and feigned interest in my undecorated Christmas tree. "I should finish this."

Her back to them, they didn't see the tears slip down Ruth's face. She cleverly wiped them away without anyone knowing she was crying at all. I had the feeling she'd become quite good at hiding her feelings. Sadly, I also had the feeling that these tears were not for me, but for the secrets she kept from Jonathan, David, Father Cliff, Ted Hagan, and everyone else in Hope Springs. She had changed, to be sure. But she didn't like *how* she'd changed.

"Jonathan, there's something important we need to talk about," Father Cliff was saying when I turned my attention back to him.

David took another sip of his coffee, but his gaze was held on Jonathan. Apparently, he knew what Father Cliff was about to say.

Jonathan looked at the two men warily. "What?"

"If you're tired—"

"I'm not tired," Jonathan said.

"It's something your father wanted," Father Cliff said carefully. "Consider it a 'last request' he had mentioned to me on several occasions. And I know it's in his will."

I looked from Father Cliff to Jonathan. My mind was blank about any last requests regarding my kids.

Father Cliff cleared his throat, glanced at David, then back at Jonathan. "He wanted you to paint something special for the church. Maybe even for Christmas. In his memory. We'll make a plaque to go with it."

"Oh," Jonathan and I said together. I had forgotten all about the idea.

Father Cliff added, "Not just for your father, but for your mother, too."

It came back to me. Being a traditional old church where nearly everything had been donated—the stained-glass windows, pews, pulpits, rooms, plaques, wall-hangings—even the tea service for the Ladies' Reading Club was a gift—I thought a painting from Jonathan would be a beautiful addition. I had mentioned it to Father Cliff several months before when I drafted my will, and had since put it out of my mind because of Jonathan's creative block.

"You're joking," Jonathan said.

"Not at all."

Jonathan stammered, "But…it's not as if I can just toss together a painting in time for Christmas.

"You've done it before," Father Cliff said. "That painting you did for the new town hall is still there—and you put that one together in less than a week. We thought it was a miracle. I still do."

Jonathan shook his head as he dropped onto the arm of the couch. “Those kinds of miracles don’t happen anymore.”

“You don’t have to answer right this minute,” Father Cliff said.

Ruth knelt down next to Jonathan. “Do it for Daddy, Jonathan.”

Jonathan glared at her.

“I told you,” David said to Father Cliff.

Father Cliff looked helplessly at Jonathan, who now looked up at his older brother.

“I told him you wouldn’t do it,” David said.

“What made you so sure I wouldn’t?”

“It’s obvious, isn’t it?”

Jonathan stood up again. “Is it? Tell me what’s obvious, David.”

David looked at him impatiently. “You’re too afraid to try. You know you wouldn’t finish it by Christmas, or Easter, or next Halloween, for that matter.”

“You’re goading me,” Jonathan said. “You’re *daring* me.”

David shrugged and drank more of his coffee. Silence hung over them like a foul odor.

Finally, Father Cliff said: “I’m just the messenger of your father’s request. Nothing says you have to do it.”

“I don’t think it’s possible. Not in such a short amount of time, what with the funeral and everything else.”

“I’m sure he has to rush back to whatever he’s doing in Phoenix,” David said.

Jonathan pressed his lips together, holding back whatever he wanted to say.

Father Cliff left it at that and said goodbye. At the door, he hesitated, and said, “It’s good to have you here—the children of Richard Lee all together again. People in this town loved him. *I* loved him, as you know. He was a good man.”

I thanked him for the impromptu eulogy, but he didn't hear me. He stepped out into the cold morning. It had begun to snow again.

Death hadn't made me a mind-reader, but I picked up some very distinct impressions about my children's thoughts, wordless messages came like waves of electricity. A disturbing sensation, particularly since they were thinking about me.

I saw myself as Jonathan saw me: a fatherly artistic impresario, one who had encouraged him with his painting with unceasing enthusiasm.

That much was true. I believed in my son's talent and affirmed him whenever I could.

Then came a darker, more oppressive perception. Jonathan felt he was a failure in my eyes for not fulfilling his artistic potential. His "artistic block" had inadvertently put a wedge between us, he thought. He imagined I had died in a state of disappointment with him.

Then, as my heart lurched from this feeling, Ruth's perceptions suddenly invaded my thoughts. To her I was a gentle, loving small-town man who was disappointed in her for leaving our small-town life in favor of big city freedom. With that, she carried a burden of guilt for the decisions she had made to get as far along in Los Angeles as she had. She had compromised her morality, done things she knew she shouldn't have done—things I wouldn't have approved of. I thought of Terry, the boy-conqueror at her apartment, and suspected that he was only one of many who—

I could go no further with that thought because David's very specific perceptions hit me like a jolt of electricity. *The people in this town loved him all right. He was a pushover for anything they wanted,* David thought.

The deep anger and cynicism of the thought took my breath away, which is an odd thing for a dead man to feel.

And then the memories flooded in. The Saturday mornings I spent helping with maintenance at the church, the various evenings I left home to visit someone who was sick in the hospital, the Knights of Columbus obligations, reading Scripture in church, the pocket-money I gave to those who sometimes came to the door for a hand-out or were destitute on the street, the charities, the civic organizations, the fund-raisers.

The time and the money, David thought. *The time and the money*...

I may have been generous to a fault, but David thought I was a gullible fool, a sucker to every worthless cause and charity that Hope Springs could throw at me.

"Now, wait just a minute—" I said, wanting to correct him—wanting to correct them all. But no one could hear me.

Ruth pressed a tissue to her nose and sniffled. "He was a good man—and a good father."

Jonathan nodded.

David remained stone-faced, saying nothing.

An uneasy feeling infiltrated my consciousness; an awareness that my perceptions of my children's lives—my relationship with them—hadn't been real.

I wondered if clarity is part of death. Do we spend our lives in a state of willful delusion and carefully contrived fantasies—and does death strip them all away? Am I now seeing things as they *really* are?

I thought about Purgatory. Was this my reckoning before I could move on?

As I looked at my three children I thought *no, this isn't Purgatory. This is Hell.*

Chapter Three

JONATHAN'S BEDROOM was in the attic. As a teenager he had announced that he wanted to move off of the second floor where the rest of us slept and get into the "loft" on his own. It appealed to his sense of artistry, he said. Kathryn wanted to encourage his *muse*, and it gave me an excuse to get rid of all the junk we'd stored there—so we obliged him.

Now, as an adult, he looked at the room with an expression of embarrassment. I even detected something in his eyes that seemed like lost hope. Little had changed since he had lived at home. The only adjustment to the room's decor was the increase of Elvis paraphernalia. I had moved the Elvis "collection" to Jonathan's room after Kathryn's death. There were photos, magazines, statuettes, collectible records, an Elvis clock with "swiveling hips" instead of a pendulum, figurines of Elvis as the young rock star, as the movie star, as the "comeback" star, as the White-Jumpsuit-Vegas star, and tons more. My inventory ranged from the tastefully luxurious to the blatantly tacky.

Jonathan wanted all the Elvis stuff in his room since he and his mother were die-hard, true-to-the-end believers, whereas I was a "fair-weather fan." I couldn't argue. Kathryn loved Elvis. Not to the degree of fanaticism that the "Elvis is still alive" disciples loved him, to be sure, but he had touched her heart like no other musician or celebrity could. She often said that there was something about his music—about *him*—that made her feel alive. I knew for a fact that she went out with me because, back in the day, I reminded her of him. The hairstyle, I mean, not the swivel in the hips.

I confess that the hairstyle was intentional. A mutual friend had told me what a big fan she was, so I made sure to wear my hair like he did. We watched *Blue Hawaii* on video on our first date. When she learned that Elvis and I shared the exact same birth date, we were as good as engaged. Then I informed her that I had served in the army at Fort Chaffee and Fort Hood—the same places Elvis had served in 1958—and that I had broken one of my fingers in a football game just like he had—and marriage was a mere formality.

I admit to being impressed by him. One of the staff officers I met—Bill Hendrix—had trained with Elvis in the army. They ate together at the canteen, went on bivouac, and learned about tanks as part of their basic training. The officer said Elvis was always friendly and polite and took the teasing about his fame good-naturedly. He was also a dutiful son who called his mother nearly every night and, later that summer, was devastated by her sudden death from hepatitis.

Bill told me how, when Elvis came back to the fort to finish his basic training after burying his mother, Bill had bumped into him one evening outside of the bunkhouse. He said Elvis looked tired and worn-out and asked, "How are you coping with your grief?"

Elvis asked, "Do you believe the dead can see what the living are doing?"

"I don't know," said Bill.

"I do," he said. "She can see me now. No more secrets from her. She can see *everything*."

For a moment Bill thought Elvis was comforted by the idea, then quickly realized that it terrified him. He walked away, his head hung low. That was the last conversation Bill had with him.

No surprise that that conversation would come back to me now.

Jonathan was right. I was a fickle fan. As much as I liked Elvis as a person, I thought his best years ended with the advent of the Beatles. After that, something changed for him. It was as if he lost his way. My wife blamed the Colonel—his manager—who let Elvis fall into the hands of corporate mercenaries. They made him commercial and forced him to make bad movies and mediocre music.

That's the easy explanation. Frankly, I believed the reasons were less obvious: something happened to him in much deeper places. What, exactly, I couldn't say. So, where Kathryn adored him to the bitter end, I held that early Elvis was the best (with a glimmer of hope during the famous "Comeback Special"). She mourned his death, I felt sorry for his lost potential.

Jonathan followed his mother's lead (and love) and took Elvis as his role model. I teased him that it wouldn't help his painting. He argued that it would, that the essence of creativity in any art form was the same.

I couldn't disagree, since I also believed, and still do, that all creativity comes from the same source: God.

Tossing his suitcase onto the bed, Jonathan scanned the room. Behind a life-size cardboard cutout of young Elvis sat his old art supplies, sketchpads, and unfinished paintings. He sat down at his student desk and looked through a scrapbook of his very first drawings. They were representations of his earliest work that Kathryn had kept for him long after he'd wanted to throw them away.

Once again, I "saw" images and felt impressions from him. They were so vivid that I couldn't tell if they were his memories or my own.

I see him as a small boy, showing me some drawings he had made.

"See, Dad? This is Mrs. McGowan's cow out in the field!"

And there is my younger self smiling. "That's wonderful, son. And what is this next to the cow, a scarecrow?"

"No!' he protests. "That's Mrs. McGowan!"

I laugh, but proudly. "A perfect likeness."

Then I see another day, a few years later. He is holding up a picture he had drawn that morning.

"This is what you drew in Sunday School today?" I ask.

"Uh huh. It's Jesus healing a blind man," my eight-year-old says excitedly. He is serious now—and wants to be taken seriously. He is no longer a child who wants to be a fireman one week and the president the next. His mind is set: he wants to be an artist. And I remember that it was his early attempts to draw Jesus's miracles in Sunday School that stirred his artist's heart. I suspect there is something inside every artist that wants to capture the miraculous, the eternal.

"I see the blind man. But why can't we see Jesus's face?" I ask earnestly.

Jonathan looks perplexed, then frowns. "It's because I *can't see Jesus's face. I... can't see it in my head," he replies sadly.*

Then I hear myself saying to him: "That's all right, son. In the movie Ben-Hur we never see Jesus's face either."

He looks at me silently. He knows I'm trying to comfort him in that well-intentioned fatherly way—and won't tolerate it. "Mrs. Ashley says I have to know *Jesus before I can draw his face."*

I nod. Mrs. Ashley is his Sunday School teacher at the Baptist church, and I wouldn't dream of contradicting her. "Knowing him in your heart is very important, but not only so you can draw him. Remember: a person is more than lines and shadows on paper. The best artists capture a sense of the person they're drawing."

That was the mystery of art: the intuitive, *spiritual* way a painter or poet or writer or composer can make lines, colors, words, rhymes, and notes come together into a form that speaks of life. I found it hard to believe that a person could be *detached* from the spiritual realm and be an artist. I often said so to Jonathan.

"Lines and shadows," the adult Jonathan said out loud to no one he could see. He tossed the scrapbook aside. "I can't even do those anymore."

Suddenly his feelings came to me like a blast of heat. He considered his life an empty canvas. It was completely blank. *What good is an empty canvas?* he mused. *What can you use it for?* He held up a sketchpad this way and that, pondering the question. *You could use it as a table, a window-shutter, a modernistic hat, a bookend.* His mind raced on in a frenzied stream of consciousness. *My paintings could be used as a tray for eggnog, a sled, a candleholder, a Christmas-tree stand...*

Then I heard my voice, something I had said to him at some point: "An empty canvas is never any good until it is used for the purpose it was created to serve." Jonathan said the words out loud, on the edge of a deep sigh.

My heart went out to him. For years I had felt like an empty canvas as well, wanting desperately to write but not having the talent to do it. It was much later—after surrendering to the truth of my limitations—that I became an editor and publisher instead.

I found contentment in helping others to write who were better than I was. But Jonathan suffered from no limitations as a painter. He could do it. I knew he could. I *willed* for him to try.

To my surprise, he picked up an empty sketchpad and started to draw.

Chapter Four

HAD IT not been for Ruth's curiosity, I wouldn't have seen what Jonathan drew then, and well into the night after he had moved from the sketchpad to a spare canvas he'd found in the closet. Why I couldn't see it, I don't know. It was as if I stood behind Jonathan while he worked and his body was always blocking my view.

Like everything else that's happened to me since I died, I can't explain why I see some things with amazing clarity while other things are kept from me.

Jonathan had declined dinner, accepting only some hot tea Ruth had brought up to him. I don't know what Ruth and David did that day. I was stuck in the loft with Jonathan, watching him work but not seeing his work. At two in the morning he stood up, turned the painting to the wall as if he couldn't bear to look at it another second, and collapsed onto his bed.

Ruth peeked in on Jonathan the next morning to see if he wanted anything from town. He was sprawled across the bed in the same position as when he'd fallen there six hours before. She had her coat on and a folded newspaper tucked under her arm. Spying the canvas on the easel, she went over to it and moved it a few inches away from the wall, then turned it for a fuller look. Now I could see it: a rough sketch of a manger surrounded by shapes and outlines of figures. *A Nativity scene?* Was that his sudden inspiration? But the number of the figures surrounding the manger was too large for any of the traditional accounts of the Birth of Christ. The shepherds and the angels? It was too early to know.

Jonathan stirred, and Ruth quickly stepped away from the canvas.

"Good morning," she said, turning to him as he labored to sit up.

"Hi." He rubbed at his face with both hands.

She tossed the folded newspaper onto the bed. "There's an article about Dad in the newspaper this morning."

Jonathan stretched and picked up the paper. A headline announced that one of Hope Springs's leading lights had died. I cringed. Next to the article was an old black-and-white photo of me, taken when I worked for one of the major publishing houses in New York. I knew immediately that this was the work of Patricia Kinney. She was a romance-writer-wanna-be who wrote features for the paper. As I glanced at the article, I saw the overblown, over-written style that was Patricia's hallmark. I thought: if I'm allowed to haunt anyone in my current state, then I might visit her tonight.

"Father Cliff wrote the obituary inside. It's sweet," Ruth said. Her eyes teared up but she blinked them away. "Do you need anything from town?"

Jonathan shook his head. "I'll go later. Do you need help with anything?"

"I have to order flowers for the funeral," she replied. "It's the one thing David didn't feel confident handling."

"Flowers are too abstract for David."

Ruth smiled, made as if to leave, then lingered at the door. "Do I still look tired?"

Jonathan squinted, trying to focus through his sleepy eyes. "You look good. The heads on Main Street will spin in every direction."

"That sounds horrific," Ruth said, then acted as if she'd only just noticed the canvas. "Oh, what's this?" She moved toward his work.

Jonathan nearly leapt from the bed to intercept her, but got tangled in the bedspread. "It's nothing," he said sharply.

She gazed at the picture as if seeing it for the first time. "I like it. Is this what you're going to paint for the church?"

"Now, Ruth . . ."

"I like the way the choir surrounds the manger," she said simply, smiled at him, then left the room.

A choir? Is that who all those people were?

Jonathan shivered and wrapped the blanket around himself. He stood up and moved to the canvas.

The cardboard cutout Elvis and I watched him curiously.

Jonathan found David downstairs in my study, surrounded by boxes stuffed with my old bank statements, canceled checks, and various documents. David hammered away at my old adding machine, cursing its stiff keys and archaic technology.

"What are you doing?" Jonathan asked from the doorway.

"It's unbelievable." The tape in the adding machine jammed up. David tossed up his hands. "I'm telling you, it's unbelievable."

"The adding machine?"

"All of this. Dad's financial situation."

"Dad was a millionaire and didn't know it?"

David tugged and jerked at the machine tape. "He might've been. But he gave it all away. If you saw the amounts—" The tape wouldn't cooperate. He pushed it all aside and took out his cell phone, I assumed to use a calculator app.

"Coffee?" Jonathan asked.

"Why did he do it?" David asked. "He could've used it for himself . . . or us."

Jonathan looked at him, a sardonic expression. "Are you saying you need something?"

"We could've lived in a better house than *this*." He waved his hand around as if gesturing to a garbage dump.

I was appalled. There was nothing wrong with our house.

"Nicer clothes instead of all those hand-me-downs," David continued. "He could have helped us through college." There was a bitterness in that last statement.

"We did okay," Jonathan said. "I had to work hard, but I made it."

"You were only studying art," David said.

Jonathan looked at him, affronted.

David didn't notice. "It was a miracle *I* made it—what with accounting and business classes. And that was only because of my scholarships. Scholarships I worked my butt off to get."

I glared at David, though he couldn't see it. He had no idea how mistaken he was. Yet, at the same instant, I felt guilty. I had made a judgement call about my children based on who I thought they were. I may have been completely wrong.

"Case in point," David continued. "Have you ever heard of the Foster Fund?"

"No."

"A lot of checks—a lot of his money—went to it."

"What is it?" Jonathan asked.

"I don't know. Some kind of charity, maybe. I couldn't find anything about it online. I'm talking *thousands* of dollars went there over the years. It looks like he started donating to it when we were in our teens and carried on up to—" He flipped through a stack of recent statements. "Well, the last check was made out a month ago."

Jonathan shrugged. "Never heard of it."

David gestured to my cluttered desk. "That's my point. He gave all this money away to something we never heard of, all while we had to struggle through school."

Jonathan leaned against the door post. "You're the only one complaining, David. Why does it matter so much? You made it, didn't you? You've got more money than you need. What's the problem?"

David leaned forward, resting his elbows on the desk. "It doesn't make sense to me."

"Why does it have to make sense?"

David shot an impatient glance at his brother. "That's just what I would've expected you to say."

Jonathan sighed. "Can't this wait? Why are you going through Dad's finances now?"

"Because I'm the executor of Dad's will. Somebody has to figure out this mess."

Jonathan looked intently at David, a telling expression on his face. "So, you'll figure it out and then rush off right after the funeral Mass—right?"

"What's the point of staying?"

Jonathan snorted and shook his head.

"We have to sell the house," David suddenly said.

"What?"

"I think we should sell the house."

"*Sell the house?*" Jonathan and I asked together.

"It'll take care of some of his outstanding bills."

I couldn't imagine what outstanding bills he was talking about. The house had been paid off years before, so was the car. I even paid off my credit cards at the end of every month. I was debt free. What outstanding bills?

"It's too soon to talk about that," Jonathan said.

David misunderstood Jonathan's concern. "We can divide equally whatever we make. It'll help you, I'm sure."

"I'm not worried about the money," Jonathan stated. "This is the house we grew up in. It's *home*."

"Whose home? Not yours, certainly not mine. Ruth's? I don't think she's interested."

"We just lost Dad. I don't want to think about losing the house, too."

David looked as if Jonathan were speaking in a foreign language. "I don't understand you. I mean, just *look at it*. Doesn't it make you feel claustrophobic?"

"You haven't seen my apartment."

David pushed away from my desk. He held his arms out to my office, to the entire house. "I don't have any attachments to this place."

"That's you."

"Are *you* planning to live here, then?"

Jonathan didn't answer the question, but said, "You didn't always feel that way. You loved this house when we were growing up. Just like I did."

David frowned.

"Don't you remember?" Jonathan asked. "It was a . . . a castle. Or a fort in the middle of the wilderness . . ."

Suddenly, as if someone had switched on a home movie, I see a young David and an even younger Jonathan playing in the living room. Both are dressed in cowboy vests, chaps, with holsters, guns, and moccasins on their feet. They chase each other around, waving their guns and shouting bang, bang, while using the furniture for cover.

"We had great adventures," I hear the adult Jonathan say, like a voice-over to the scene I see. "You liked to be Daniel Boone."

"Davey Crockett," the adult David corrects him.

The adult Jonathan says, "I was Davey Crockett. No—wait—you liked to be that Texas Ranger."

"Wrong," the adult David says. "You were the Texas Ranger."

"No," the adult Jonathan says.

"Yes. You liked wearing the Texas Ranger hat."

The adult Jonathan grunts. "Maybe I did."

"And I played with the rifle" the adult David says.

"Hold on. No. You had the pistol. I had the rifle," says the adult Jonathan.

The two adults now get into an argument about who was who and who owned what, and I smile because the scene is so clear in front of me. David wears a Texas cowboy hat and holds a pistol while Jonathan wears a coonskin cap and carries a toy rifle.

What am I to make of this? I'm seeing a memory that must be my own—I certainly remember seeing the boys running around like that—yet it is called to my mind in perfect clarity by their recollections. And even though they are confused about what they remember, I see it as it really was. What does it mean?

Slowly, the scene fades to black, and I am standing in my study again.

David sat up in my chair and said firmly, "You're being sentimental. We were *kids* then. We're not kids anymore. This place is no castle. Our memories have nothing to do with us now."

"Of course they do."

"Maybe for you," David said.

Jonathan jabbed a finger in the air at David. "For you, too. You're lying to yourself if you say they don't."

"You're going to be my therapist now?"

"That would be a bigger job than I could handle." Jonathan turned away and walked to the kitchen.

David was on his feet, following him. "Meaning what?"

"Meaning that you've turned into something I simply don't understand." Jonathan was at the counter. He picked up the coffee pot and poured out what little liquid remained inside.

"Turned *into* something?" David asked. "Like some kind of *monster*? Why—because I'm successful? Is that what bugs you?"

"I don't care about your success. I'm not consumed by it the way you are," Jonathan replied. "I'm talking about something else."

"Spill it out."

Jonathan turned to face him. "I'm talking about... what you've become."

"What *I've* become?" David was derisive now. "Maybe we should talk about what you *haven't* become."

I flinched on Jonathan's behalf. My two sons glared at each other for a moment.

Jonathan put the coffee pot down and headed for the door at the other end of the kitchen. "I'm done with this. I'm going out."

"Going out for what?" David asked, taunting him. "Art supplies? Feeling inspired? Ruth said you started a painting. Do you think you'll finish this one?"

"No comment," Jonathan growled as he stormed out.

"You won't," David called after him, a smug expression on his face. "You never do."

If David weren't so old and I weren't so dead, I would've been tempted to slap him.

David went back to my office and stood over the mess of paperwork. He picked up an old check and turned it over and over. "Foster Fund," he said softly.

Chapter Five

MY CURRENT position—being dead, I mean—allows me to appreciate the town of Hope Springs with new eyes. Established in the late 1800s, it quickly became a stopping point for trains headed southwest from Denver. The nearby Rocky Mountains provided mining of various types to give the town its industry in the early twentieth century. People came from all over the country to enjoy the natural hot springs.

The downtown grew from a few shacks that served as hardware and feed stores, a single hotel, a saloon, and bank, to more prosperous looking red-bricked and gray-stoned businesses. Then, like so many towns, the mining moved elsewhere, the central businesses of the town declined, and the inevitable economic slump lasted almost two decades. Small shops became government welfare offices. Hayes Department Store, with its five stories, old-fashioned elevator, and red-jacketed operator, succumbed to the chain stores at the mall and the factory-outlets that sprung up towards Denver. Hayes was gutted and turned into a massive consignment assembly for fly-by-night merchants needing a cheap site to sell their stuff.

For me the litmus test for the town was the Coliseum Cinema. Built in 1939, it was big-screened, balconied, ornate, and, later, "air conditioned"—a proud venue, equal to any theatre in a larger city. *Gone with the Wind* was the first movie it screened. By the 1970s the theatre looked worn out; the red curtains faded, the velvet wallpaper peeled, the cushions on the seats split. A multi-plex cinema opened at the new mall outside of town and the Coliseum closed. Disney's *Herbie the Love Bug* was the last movie screened there. What a sad way to go out.

A Pentecostal church rented it for nearly a decade. Then it sat derelict, an eyesore in the middle of Main Street.

The health-craze of the latter part of the twentieth century revitalized the town. People suddenly remembered that we had mountains and a ski resort opened up in the winter. The various lakes and streams brought in fishing enthusiasts. Hiking trails were in abundance and people wearing expensive shoes, shorts, shirts, and backpacks arrived. New houses were built to accommodate them, if only for various seasons. Hayes Department Store was turned into condos. Abandoned stores became boutique shops.

Just before Thanksgiving I'd heard a rumor that someone wanted to renovate the Coliseum and open it as an "Art House" cinema. This gave me hope—until I later learned that Bev Tyler was spreading the rumor because she'd overheard someone tell Wilkie Bell at the diner that "someone should renovate the place and open it as an 'Art House' cinema."

That someone was me.

I seriously considered the idea.

There was something about the snowfall from last night that made the town look like its former self—reminding me of the old black-and-white photos of the 1940s Hope Springs that George Ferber still has hanging in his dry-cleaners. Even the old-fashioned Christmas decorations that the city has been putting up for years carried a certain charm in spite of the cracked and peeling silver on the bells, the chips in the gold chains, and the frayed green on the metal wreaths hung on the lampposts. I half-expected to see the lights of the Coliseum's marquee light up again.

Ruth, bundled in her foreign name-brand coat and scarf, strolled along Main Street with me as her unseen companion. She had a forced smile on her lovely face. I could tell she was glad to be back in a familiar place, her home for most of her life, but was intimidated by its potential to make her feel things she didn't want to feel. She said hello to Toni what's-her-name, someone she was on the high school yearbook committee with. She waved happily to Donna you-know-who, the one that everyone thought would be a model but now worked at the daycare center.

There was a moment of genuine warmth when Patricia Gnoffino rounded a corner, pushing her twins in a stroller, and nearly knocked Ruth over. They were never close friends, but time made them realize how much they'd liked each other after all. They embraced there on the street. Ruth made a fuss about the twins while Patricia made a fuss about my death, and they parted with promises to meet for coffee whenever Ruth could find the time. Others walked past— people who knew me mostly—to say how sorry they were about my passing. "He's with the Lord now," Dolly Edwards said as she patted Ruth's arm with a wrinkled hand. Ruth smiled.

In Sunshine Florists, Ruth was disheartened to find Jan Binnocek working behind the counter.

"It's so good to see you again," Jan lied. "You look terrific. Maybe a little tired. Losing your father like that must be so hard."

Ruth nodded graciously and asked about flowers for my funeral. Jan pulled out several brochures and plastic-lined catalogues filled with photos of various bouquets and costs. Ruth eventually selected an arrangement of lilies to place next to my casket. I never cared much for lilies, but Ruth loved them. Flowers are more for the living than the dead.

Ruth thanked Jan for her help and returned to the crisp arctic day outside. From the front of the florist shop, Ruth saw a shop called "Hagan's Hand-Picked Books & Coffee." Ted Hagan's shop. She debated whether or not to drop by. I knew her heart said yes, but her pride said no.

The decision was wrenched away from her when Ted himself suddenly appeared next to her. She almost didn't recognize him: he was dressed in a long black overcoat and flat cap and sported a beard she had never seen. He was over six foot and towered over her five-foot-five frame.

"Donna Milton came in the bank and said she saw you," Ted said with a shy smile. He was a good, wholesome-looking boy with sharp blue eyes and curly brown hair. "She said you were buying flowers for your dad."

"I was just thinking about you," Ruth smiled. "I saw your new shop. But I hate to bother people when they're working."

"It's no bother. Didn't Father Cliff give you my message?"

Ruth nodded. "Yes, he did. But—well—you know."

"I know this is a difficult time, and there are plenty of things to arrange. I'm going to miss your father a lot. But if you have a few minutes to come to the shop for the best hot coffee you'll find on a cold winter's day... or any day, actually... that is, if you don't have other errands to run..." Ted was rambling. It was something he always did when he was nervous.

Ruth was relieved that he hadn't suggested going to Michelle's Ice Cream parlor, if only to avoid the awkwardness of re-creating their relationship by sitting in their "favorite booth" as they had so often after classes. She didn't know that the booth was gone, the casualty of a major renovation at the place where it went from a "Gay Nineties" look to a 1950s diner style.

"Let's go," Ruth said, looking up at him. I saw the flicker of a light in her eyes and a real smile on her lips. *She still thinks his nervousness is cute.*

Ted's shop had a large front window filled with a display of first editions of classic books. They walked in and Ted led her to the right where the café covered half of the ground floor. He'd put in a hardwood floor with a variety of wooden tables and chairs. There was a large pot-belly stove in the middle of the floor. At the far end was an old-fashioned bar Ted had bought from the Royal Hotel when it was renovated a year ago. The bar was a mix of dark wood and gold framing. Behind it the barista—a kid named Justin Pierce—worked the various machines that lined a large decorative mirror, which also came from the Royal. A lone woman I didn't recognize read a newspaper at a corner table.

Ruth stopped in the middle of the floor and looked around. The walls of the ground floor were filled with books—meticulously arranged by subject—and tables were covered with books of special interest or on sale. A cash register and sundry stationary pads, tablets, pens, and cards sat on another long counter at the back wall. To the left was a wide staircase that led to the second floor, part of which could be seen as a balcony above her. More shelves and tables of books.

"Very nice," Ruth said.

Ted gestured to one of the tables and held the chair for her. She sat down and pushed her coat back onto her chair. He took his place across from her. I noticed that Ted was playing Elvis in the background: "Blue Christmas."

"She started working there . . . oh, a year ago?" Ted said in answer to a question I didn't hear Ruth ask.

"Imagine my surprise. I had no idea Jan Binnocek knew the first thing about flowers," Ruth said.

"She took some kind of course at the community college."

"I thought she was going to cosmetology school," said Ruth. "Hair and makeup to . . . flowers?"

Ted shrugged. "Beauty is beauty, whether human or floral, I guess."

"Uh huh," Ruth said skeptically. "The lilies I ordered might wind up looking like dreadlocks."

"Do you want something to drink?"

"A coffee, since you said it's the best," Ruth said.

Ted flagged Justin at the counter and ordered for them both. Silence prevailed until Ted said softly, "It's not going to be the same, you know."

"What?"

"Hope Springs. Without your father." Ted fiddled with a packet of sugar he'd retrieved from the small bowl in the center of the table. "He used to meet me here on Wednesday mornings."

Ruth was surprised. "You spent a lot of time with him?"

"A little. We'd meet here, or I'd go over to his house on Friday nights."

"To do what?"

"To talk. Maybe play a board game. Then talk some more." Ted cleared his throat. "He said that just because we'd broken up, there was no reason I couldn't still be part of the family."

Ruth smiled sadly. "It was very sweet of you to spend time with him. But didn't it cut in on your social life?"

"That *was* my social life," Ted replied, and his cheeks turned color.

"You don't expect me to believe that. I'm sure you have your share of Hope Springs girls scratching at your door." Ruth paused for a second to think about what she'd just said. "Maybe that wasn't the best expression to use."

"No girls come scratching or pounding or texting or whatever it is girls do now. I guess they figure I'm not worth having after you left me," Ted said.

Ruth rolled her eyes. "Oh, please."

"You think I'm kidding?"

"I'm not sure I want to know," she said, glancing away as Justin brought their coffees. Silence as she tasted the coffee. She nodded her approval. "This *is* good."

Ted doctored his cup with a sweetener and a splash of half-and-half. "I'm not really much of a coffee drinker," he said. "Justin picks the roasts."

"Then why did you—?" Ruth started to say, then smiled as if she might laugh.

"Books and coffee," Ted replied, as if the answer was obvious.

"Is the beard part of your overall bookstore-coffee-owner look?" Ruth teased.

Ted touched his beard self-consciously. "Don't you approve?"

Ruth leaned over her coffee and cupped the mug in both hands, but her eyes were on Ted. She scrutinized his face. "Yes, I approve."

"Good."

There was an old-fashioned radiator in front of the display window. The glass steamed.

"Why don't you tell me about Dad? What did you talk about on your Friday nights together?" she asked.

"Lots of things." Ted looked at her directly. "You."

Ruth squirmed. "Ted—"

"You asked," Ted said. "Your father and I both missed you. We talked about how you were doing. We wished you would come home." He took a sip of his coffee. A drop of it hung to his beard. Without thinking, Ruth reached up with a napkin and wiped it away. He smiled. "Why don't you? Come home, I mean."

"It's not that easy."

"Sure it is."

"No, it isn't," she said firmly.

I got certain impressions from my daughter, but they were all tangled up. She felt she couldn't come home because she didn't think she was *worthy* to come home. She felt guilty for the ways she'd compromised herself in Los Angeles. *You don't know me, Ted,* she thought. *You think I'm the same girl who left three years ago. But I'm not. You don't know me.*

Ted watched her carefully. "You just decide to come home and do it. What's so hard about that?"

"You don't know. Things are complicated. *Life* is complicated."

"Not when you're doing the right thing with your life."

Ruth's anger rose, and she sat up. "That's very cute. Very clever. Is that one of those small-town platitudes you picked up at church?"

"Don't get mad, I just meant that—"

"Tell me something. Why would I want to come back to *Hope Springs,* of all places? Especially now that my dad won't be here?"

"What's wrong with Hope Springs?" Ted asked defensively.

"It's so . . . so small."

"You have a problem with small towns?"

I groaned. A small town wasn't Ruth's problem. It was merely a diversion. I knew it, but Ted didn't.

"Come on, Ted," Ruth went on. "It's depressing. Nobody comes downtown any more. They're all out at the mall. And it's a second-rate mall, at best."

"So, Los Angeles has first-rate malls. Big deal. Is that your criteria for where you live? Malls? What about family and friendship and community and a sense of belonging . . . ?"

"Big cities have those things."

"For you? Are you really happy there? Tell me about your friends in Los Angeles."

The question startled Ruth. She wondered how much Ted really knew about her life. Had I guessed at things and passed them onto him during our friendly Friday night conversations? Of course, I hadn't. Her life in Los Angeles was a mystery to me. But she didn't know that, and it scared her.

"I don't want to talk about this," Ruth said.

Ted saw her expression and wisely retreated. "I'm sorry, Ruth. It's just that . . . I worry about you. I want to believe you're happy, but, at the same time, I hope you aren't. I . . . " He stammered. "I'm making a mess of this."

"Ted, Hope Springs isn't my home anymore. My brothers have moved away, my mother is gone, so is my father now—there's nothing here for me."

Ted stared at his coffee and chewed the inside of his lip. It's what he did when he had something to say but didn't know how to say it; he stared and chewed. I recognized the quirk. So did Ruth. He didn't see her gentle smile.

Then she suddenly stood up, the chair scraping against the floor. "I should go."

Ted was also on his feet and nearly knocked the table over in the process. Her purse fell to the floor, the contents spilling out. They both knelt down, scrambling to shove everything back in.

When the job was done he had a pained expression that I couldn't interpret. Ruth didn't notice it.

"I'd like to see you again," Ted said.

"I don't know. We have so much to do...for the funeral. You know."

"Still. If you didn't rush back to LA," Ted said.

Ruth put on her coat. "Thank you for spending so much time with Dad."

"Your father was good to me," Ted said softly, a hitch in his voice. "It was the very least I could ever have done."

"It was more than I did," Ruth said, then quickly turned and walked to the door.

Chapter Six

JONATHAN ALSO went to town—to the Colorama Art Store—and bought the necessary supplies to work on the painting for me. His heart still wasn't in it, but he had an idea, a single compelling idea, and that was more than he'd had in a long time.

I had seen artistic block in a few of the writers I had worked with over the years. It seemed like a remarkably misunderstood phenomenon to me. In some cases, the artist had no ideas at all. In other cases, the artist had plenty of ideas but couldn't decide which one to focus on.

Jonathan thought he had a compelling idea now and had worked feverishly on it throughout the morning. Now, even as he despaired of his work, he told himself that he was doing the painting for me—because I'd requested it—or because he was trying to work out his grief. I didn't care either way. I was glad he was painting again.

I couldn't see clearly what he was doing. Not since Ruth's look earlier in the day. My view was blocked partly by Jonathan. I wondered why. Who chooses these vantage points for me? Why couldn't I see it on my own last night, but saw it clearly when Ruth came into the room—or now as David knocked on the door and peeked in?

Jonathan was sitting on a stool in front of the canvas, busy with his work. "Go away," he said to David.

"Mrs. Wagner brought a stew for us to eat," David said.

"Great."

"People from St. Clare's have been bringing food all day."

"That's nice," Jonathan said without really listening.

"Father Cliff is here. We're going to discuss the insurance."

"Good."

"Then maybe we'll decorate the Christmas tree."

"Uh huh."

"Then we might set it on fire."

"Good."

"Along with the rest of the house. We'll need you for skin grafts, of course."

"Right."

"If there are any survivors."

"Sure."

"You're not listening to me," David said, then stepped fully into the room. I then saw the painting more fully. The group of people that Ruth had thought was a choir was not—or, I should say, it didn't look like any choir I'd ever seen. The roughly sketched figures looked more like an odd collection of people of different ages, nationalities, and vocations. The clothes, uniforms, and hairstyles also gave me the impression that they represented different time periods throughout history. I was reminded of the cover to the Beatles' *Sgt. Pepper's Lonely Hearts Club Band* album. Father Cliff would be pleased. He was a big Beatles fan. We often had the "Beatles versus Elvis" argument. That's as much as I got to see before Jonathan stood up, blocking my view. He dropped a gray tarp over his work.

"I want to see it," David said and took a step towards the canvas.

"No. Only when it's finished."

"Will I live so long?" he asked. It was a challenge. Then he left the room.

Jonathan froze where he was, then slowly turned and stared at the tarp. His features stiffened. He threw a paintbrush into the holding tray. He looked at the cardboard Elvis with an expression that asked, "Did your family ever treat you like this?"

In the living room David was back in his element as he and Father Cliff finished double-checking and signing various legal and insurance forms. Father Cliff looked better than he had yesterday; less tired and less grief-stricken. The "business" of being a priest helped. I got the impression or possibly heard him humming "In My Life" by the Beatles. He'd been listening to it repeatedly until it buried itself in his subconscious and now recycled itself whenever he wasn't thinking about anything in particular.

I was aware that my death had affected him at another level, beyond the loss of a close friend. It reminded him that he was getting older and many of his closest and dearest friends had left or were leaving him behind. I sensed that his faith in God is being tested by a fear of loneliness. And he prayed to God again and again not to let him live past any obvious usefulness. God's response is not one that I can hear from my present position.

"Thank you for all you've done," David said to Father Cliff. He flipped over the last page of a long legal document. Business was concluded. "I appreciate your help with all the arrangements and details."

Father Cliff cocked an eyebrow at the formality of David's tone. "You're welcome."

"When all of his accounts are settled, I'd like to make sure you get a little something for all your work. You or the church. You decide." David shoved his gold pen into his shirt pocket.

"I don't want anything from you, David," Father Cliff said firmly. "I'm doing this for your father."

David picked up the tone in Father Cliff's voice. "Suit yourself. It wouldn't have been very much anyway. Not the way my dad handled money."

Father Cliff frowned. "I disagree. Your father had a good head for money."

David grunted.

"You don't believe me?" asked the priest.

"I've been going over his finances," said David. "'A good head for money' is not a phrase I'd use about my father."

Father Cliff sat back in my easy chair and folded his arms. "Granted, he wasn't the success that you are—at least, not the way the world defines success."

"No argument there," David chuckled.

"But don't you think your father was rich in a far more important way?" Father Cliff asked. "He was rich in goodness, in people."

David leveled a cool gaze at Father Cliff. "I'd say that a lot of people around here were rich from my father's goodness."

"That's how your father wanted it. 'You only take with you those things that you give away,'" Father Cliff said.

"I don't remember that Bible verse."

"It's not a Bible verse," Father Cliff stated. "It was in the movie *It's a Wonderful Life*. George Bailey had it hanging on his office wall—next to a photo of his father. But, by your standard, George Bailey was a failure, too."

"I never liked that movie," David said. "Tell me, Father, what do you know about the Foster Fund?"

Father Cliff unsuccessfully masked his surprise. "Why? What about it?"

"My father gave a lot of money to it, and I'd like to know more about his investment."

I was curious to see how Father Cliff would skate around the inquiry without appearing suspicious. "It wasn't an 'investment,' as you use the word."

"Tell me about it."

Father Cliff shuffled in his chair. "Your father was a responsible man. Why are you so concerned about who he gave his money to?"

David maintained his poker-faced expression. "It makes a lot of difference to me when, for years, I've tried to figure out why my father did what he did with his money—why my father did a lot of the things he did. Knowing the answer might help me."

"David, do you really think you'll understand your father better if you can sort out his bank statements and his accounting practices? Is that what you're really after?"

"Isn't it in the Bible that where a man's treasure is, that's where his heart is, too?"

Father Cliff met the challenge. "Try to remember that, while a stack of cancelled checks and receipts may be an *indicator* of your father's character, they're not the final measurement of who he was as a man. They're still only numbers and piles of paper that'll turn yellow and crumple into dust one day."

Just then the front door was thrown open. "Hello?" Ruth shouted from the other room.

David and Father Cliff went out to meet her.

Her arms were burdened with groceries and clothes boxes. "Did you see? It's snowing again. It's beautiful out there," she said as she blew through to the kitchen.

Father Cliff watched her go, then reached for the coat rack. "I have to be going," he said and put on his black overcoat. "Don't forget: I'll need the list of hymns for the Mass."

"We'll get them to you," David said.

"If there's anything else you need before tomorrow, just let me know." Father Cliff put on his gloves. He looked thoughtful. "David, if you want to know your father, then you have to know the Faith that he knew. The measure of a man isn't in a box of receipts or even the box we'll bury him in. The measure of a man is in here." Father Cliff tapped his chest. "A changed heart."

After Father Cliff left, David went to the window and looked out at the falling snow. "Trite," he muttered.

Ruth was banging around in the kitchen, and David wandered to the undecorated Christmas tree. On a nearby table, a photo of Elvis peered up at him from the cover of the *Elvis' Christmas Album*—the original red one with Elvis's face surrounded by presents and Christmas decorations.

Ruth started to sing "Blue Christmas" in the kitchen.

"You're surprisingly chipper," David called out to her.

"I dreaded going to town but it turned out all right," Ruth said as she returned from the kitchen and hung up her coat.

I was surprised. When she left Ted, she was upset. Had something happened in the meantime?

"I don't know why, but I feel pretty good," she said.

"It's possible to feel like that when you're not hungover," David said with a smirk.

Ruth scowled at him.

"Did you meet up with Teddy bear?" David asked. He wasn't going to let anything go.

"Yes, and we had coffee at his new shop."

"And?"

"And *what*?"

"What did you talk about?"

"Not much," she said. "He spent a lot of time with Dad. And he wants me to move back."

"You're kidding," David laughed. "Now there's a joke."

"Why?"

"Seriously, Ruth. You—back in Hope Springs?"

To hear her own words and attitude come from David's mouth was annoying. She brushed past him and went to the boxes of Christmas decorations.

"What do you mean?"

"You're too sophisticated for this town now."

"Is that what I am: *sophisticated*?"

"What would *you* call yourself?"

Grabbing one of the boxes, she pulled it out to the center of the floor. "I'm still trying to figure that one out."

"Be serious, Ruth," David said. "You've moved on to bigger and better things. You'd suffocate here."

"What makes you so sure I'm not suffocating in Los Angeles?"

"You probably are, but that's from their traffic jams. I'm talking about something else."

"Like what?" She sat next to the box and stared up at him.

He looked at her as if the need to explain himself was ridiculous. "Well..."

"Well what?" She handed him a green Christmas ball from the box.

"It's so *backwards* here." He hung the ball on the tree. "You know what I mean. It's a way of life no one lives anymore. It's innocent to the point of absurdity. You're past that."

"I'm past being innocent?" she asked.

David threw her a warning glance. "Do you really want me to answer that question? Do I have to remind you of the weekend I was in LA on business, and we met up with those friends of yours? Remember the party you said I *had* to attend? Do you—*can* you—remember anything at all?"

Ruth shoved the box and the ornaments rattled loudly. I was afraid they'd break.

David continued, "Ted has the look of a guy who should have become a priest. He's all innocence. You two probably never went past first base when you dated."

Ruth said nothing. Her hands gripped the edge of the box.

David knelt down next to her. "He still thinks you're that girl—sweet and pure. Do you really think you can maintain that illusion? Do you think he'll feel the same about you if he found out about your life in LA?"

"When did you become so cynical?" Ruth asked and shoved another ornament into his hands.

"When did you become so naive?" he replied and put the ornament on the tree. "A town like Hope Springs might be charming on a day like today, when the snow makes it look like a Norman Rockwell painting. But to live here indefinitely? Not a chance. You'll go crazy. What could you possibly like about it?"

"The innocence you just dismissed, for one thing," Ruth said sharply. "They still put a nativity scene on the city hall lawn. That's against the law in Los Angeles."

"Nativity scenes? Is that what you want?"

"As I walked down the street, people kept stopping me to say how sorry they were to hear about Dad. I had forgotten how..." She searched for the right words. "I'd forgotten how *human* people can be."

"Just like a scene out of *It's A Wonderful Life*, right?" David turned to her. "George Bailey with an armload of newspapers about his brother's war medals. The town gathers to rejoice."

"Something like that."

"This isn't Bedford Falls, Ruth."

"Yes it is," Ruth said. "And you're Mr. Potter."

"Oh, please," he said wearily. "Is that how it is? The successful older brother gets pegged as Mr. Potter? Or maybe I should be Ebenezer Scrooge."

"Either one sounds right to me." She angrily pushed the box of ornaments towards him. "Here. Finish the job."

"Why should I do it?"

"We have to decorate the tree before the guests arrive tomorrow."

"Guests? What guests?" he asked. "I don't want any guests."

I laughed. They were playing out a scene from the very movie David said he hated.

"Everyone's coming over after the funeral Mass," Ruth explained.

"Since when?"

"It's tradition!"

"Whose tradition?" David said with a growl. "It's not *my* tradition."

"They started it when great-grandma died."

"That's ridiculous," he said.

"And don't you remember after Mom died?"

"No."

"Oh, that's right," she said sarcastically. "You had to go back to New York right after the funeral. Business as usual."

David stared at her. He looked genuinely perplexed by her attitude. "There wasn't anything here to be done."

"Except console Dad."

"Right," he scoffed. "I would've been good at that."

"You'll never know, will you?" she growled and gave him a steely look. "Anyway, it's already arranged. It's probably best that way. You, me, and Jonathan, grieving alone together, we'd probably kill each other in the process."

David shook his head. "I don't want a lot of strange people coming over."

"Strange people? David, a lot of these folks used to be our friends."

"No—they were *your* friends and *Dad's* friends. They weren't mine." He gave the box of ornaments a gentle kick.

Why were they taking their anger out on my poor ornaments?

"You make me so mad when you get like this," Ruth said. "If it weren't for the funeral Mass and what's left of the Christmas spirit, I'd give you a black eye."

She pushed the box at him and stormed out of the room and into the kitchen. A banging of pans commenced.

"Wait a minute," David called after her. "I'm *not* decorating this tree. Ruth!"

She didn't answer. With his hands on his hips, David stood for a moment. His eyes moved indecisively between the empty tree and the box of ornaments. Fuming, he pulled out a box of lights, which I'd carefully put away the year before. I hated tangled light-cords and had wrapped this string around a large piece of cardboard.

He slowly unraveled the cord and then stood in front of the tree again. "Why did you have me put on the ornaments before we put on the lights?" he shouted.

He took the ornaments off of the tree again and began a slow rotation to put the lights on the branches.

Suddenly he fades—or the scene dissolves, to use the film term—and I now see a younger version of myself putting the lights on the tree. Kathryn is nearby unpacking another box of Christmas balls and my heart lurches at the sight of her. Kathryn. She looks so real, so vibrant and alive. I wish—beg—for my younger self to turn and take her in his arms. Hold her close right this minute and tell her how much he loves her, how much he can't live without her. But my younger self carries on with the task at hand.

Where is she now, I wonder with a tearful ache. Why am I experiencing this mess with my family alone? Will we be reunited again?

The answers aren't forthcoming and the scene continues. Kathryn is pulling out the Christmas balls. David and Jonathan as children are playfully wrapping Ruth, who is barely walking, in silver tinsel. She giggles with delight.

I can feel the warmth and the love even in this faraway place.

The scene of domestic bliss is interrupted by someone knocking at the front door. Young David runs to answer it. He is surprised to see a stranger standing there, hat in hand. David frowns. He knows what the man wants. With undisguised boredom, he calls for me. I go to the front door and recognize the man. J.P. Coleman is his name. He was laid-off from the coal mines the year before. He and his family have been in dire straits ever since.

Now I realize that this is David's memory I'm seeing, and not mine, for I meet J.P. on the porch while my point-of-view stays near David. He watches as I give the man some money for food. His expression is one of deep distrust and resentment.

After J.P. leaves, I mess up David's hair as I return to the tree. He looks up at me with a frown that, at the time, I didn't see.

The home-movie seems to run out to a white screen, then suddenly switches to another scene. The look of the family and the living room is much the same as the previous scene. The kids are the same ages as before, so are Kathryn and I. But the room is now cluttered with unwrapped gifts, and children in their pajamas are in the throes of Christmas-morning excitement.

Kathryn and I sit on the couch, she in a new robe and I in trousers and a T-shirt adorned with a new tie. Jonathan and Ruth are over-the-moon with what they find behind the tree. For Ruth, a nice rocking horse. For Jonathan, a beginner's paint set, complete with an easel and a box of paints. David tears into a large box, tearing down the sides so we can all see a small metal car—modeled after a flashy red Stingray. At first he is overjoyed and nearly kills himself climbing in. Then his expression changes as his feet hit something he didn't expect. The car has pedals. He looks up at me.

"But I wanted one with an electric motor—like the one in the catalogue!" he says.

"It was too expensive," I explain. "This one is just as nice—better exercise, too," I add as a half-joke.

David holds onto the steering wheel, jerking it back and forth angrily. "But I want the electric one."

"David," Kathryn rebukes him.

"I'm sorry, son. We couldn't afford it," I say.

Suddenly I see in David's mind a vision of J.P. getting money from me at the front door. He makes the connection between me giving money away and our not being able to afford the play car that he wanted.

"You can't have everything you want," my younger self says, which seems to add insult to injury, unbeknownst to me.

"Yes, I can!" he shouts as he rushes from the room.

At the time, to my mortal eyes and sensibilities, I thought it was an incidental moment—David throwing a tantrum because of his disappointment about the car. But I see now how it proved to be formative in ways that much larger and more seemingly significant moments weren't.

I remember after my father died I found a box full of his journals in the attic. He'd kept them all the way back to his childhood. They were filled with brief notations about the activities and events of the day: he'd gone to the dentist, the price of bread and milk had gone up, they'd had a heat wave one particular August. Rarely did he mention the doings of our politicians in Washington or the conflicts abroad. His life was filled with incidentals, not history-shaking events. Yet those incidentals were often profound in their impact. A scribbled note from his teenage years said simply: "Valentine's banquet tonight at church." That was where he met my mother. There was his notation on a day much later in his life:

"Dr. Benson—have eyes checked." That eye exam brought the doctor's attention to some irregularities that led to the discovery of a malignant brain tumor. He died from it.

Perhaps in life there are no incidentals.

Back at the Christmas tree, the grown-up David stopped to look at how he'd arranged the string of lights. But his mind was not on the lights. *"Was it too much to ask?"* he asked no one.

I tried with all my might to answer him, wanting to shake the tree, move a piece of furniture, do something that might let him know that I was nearby, that I knew, that I understood.

Nothing moved. He did not hear me. Instead, he pushed the play-button on a nearby CD player, and Elvis sang "If Every Day Was Like Christmas."

"Elvis," David groaned. "Doesn't he have any Nat King Cole around here?"

Chapter Seven

JONATHAN HAD fallen asleep. He was fully dressed and stretched across the bed. I had to wonder if he always slept in his clothes.

Ruth, still angry with David, peeked in on him. She smiled at the disheveled lump on the bed, and I couldn't help but feel the enormous love she felt behind her smile. I got a clear sense of a bond between the two of them that neither of them ever had with David. I often blamed it on David's stubborn aloofness. But I now understand that it was more than mere personal differences: Ruth and Jonathan had an unspoken empathy, a bonding of the heart that could never be pinpointed to personalities or social circumstances or upbringing. It was—dare I say it?—something mystical.

Ruth ventured near the covered canvas. She lifted the cover as quietly as she could and saw how the work was taking shape. I could see that Jonathan had finished the sketch of the crowd and had even begun adding the colors. There was no doubt now that the crowd was a representation of a multitude of people from different countries and walks of life.

I remembered that Norman Rockwell once did a painting around the same idea. But this was no Norman Rockwell. This was in the style of Jonathan Lee—a sparse style where only a few lines and the simplest of colors conveyed meaning beyond the obvious. *Minimalist* is the word some artists would use.

The diverse crowd was gathered around a manger scene. There was no mistaking Mary and Joseph, the shepherds, and the Wise Men as they knelt before the makeshift crib. But the baby in the crib was unfinished. The baby's arms and legs were exposed, reaching upwards as newborn limbs are inclined to do, but the baby's face was merely a circle.

"Get away from that," Jonathan snapped from the bed.

Ruth jerked the cover back in place. "Why?" she asked, startled. "It's beautiful, Jonathan. It's wonderful."

"It's not finished!" He struggled to sit up. His head hung down as if he bore a cross on his shoulders I couldn't see. "I can't finish it."

Ruth sat on the edge of the bed next to him. "Why can't you?"

He closed his eyes wearily. "I tried everything I could. The baby Jesus . . . nothing would work. I couldn't paint him. I knew all along I couldn't do it."

"What are you talking about? It's a baby. Just paint a baby."

"It's not just any baby. It's the baby *Jesus*."

Ruth frowned, "Jonathan—now isn't the time to be the temperamental artist."

Jonathan shook his head. "It's useless. I was ready to toss the whole thing into a fire."

"No."

"It's terrible."

"You *can't*!" Ruth insisted. "Promise me, Jonathan. Promise you won't hurt that painting."

Jonathan brooded silently.

"If you don't promise, I'll take it with me. I won't leave the room without it."

Jonathan considered the threat for a moment, then nodded slowly.

"Finish it, Jonathan. You can. I believe in you. Just like Daddy always believed in you."

He didn't answer her.

Knowing she could do no more, she moved towards the door. "I have your word," she said.

Jonathan nodded again and Ruth left.

Looking at the covered painting, Jonathan sighed deeply. There were tears in his eyes.

Ruth wandered like a ghost through the house. She felt badly for Jonathan in the attic and was annoyed with David in the living room. Where was she to go? She considered reading in her room, but the decor—unchanged since she'd left—was too much of a reminder of her past life. She browsed through various novels in the hallway bookcase and on the shelves in my office. Nothing appealed to her.

She searched haphazardly. I suspected she was really looking for something about her mother or me, a photo she hadn't seen before, a diary or journal that might give her a revelation about our past.

I thought of my own father's journals. When I'd found them in the attic, I naturally looked for the day I was born, just to see if he'd written anything to mark the occasion. He had. "Baby boy born at 10:30. Red and wrinkled. I'm so proud." That was all. But it meant more to me than if he'd written an entire book about how much he loved me. Now, as Ruth poked around, I wished I had kept journals for her to find.

She decided on a book by Henri Nouwen that I hadn't had a chance to read—*The Return of the Prodigal Son*—and I wondered if the title resonated with her feelings. She went into the bathroom to have a hot bath. Unlike modern tubs that are really only useful as shower stalls, our tub was an old-fashioned claw-footed monster that a person could easily stretch out in. Kathryn used to say that the tension simply dissolved away in that tub. Ruth followed her mother's lead.

It would have been creepy beyond words had I been unable to leave. But, thankfully, I was suddenly standing in the living room where David had finished putting the lights on the tree but given up on doing anything more. He paced now, not because of his argument with Ruth, but memories of Christmases past. Elvis sang in the background, though David insisted on humming Nat King Cole's "Christmas Song" as if in battle. The juxtaposition of the two singers and their incompatible styles was unbearable. I was rescued by a knock at the door.

David was certain it was another casserole, soufflé, or crock-pot of stew from some well-meaning member of my parish. He scowled, crossed the room and opened the door with an artificial smile in place. Ted Hagan stood there, carrying nothing more than a sled. He was dusted with snow as if he'd fallen off once too often. His cheeks were ruddy and his eyes were wide, watery, and filled with life.

"Hi, David," Ted said sheepishly. "Is Ruth here?"

"Uh huh," David replied, scanning Ted from head to foot.

"I've been sledding with Dale Johnson and his kids," Ted explained as he tried to knock the snow off his coat, trousers, and boots.

David gestured. "Come in."

Ted started through the door.

"Leave the sled outside."

"Oh," Ted said, embarrassed, and put the sled on the porch. He dusted himself off then stepped inside, hanging up his coat, scarf, and hat. He sat down on the couch while David called up the stairs for Ruth.

"She'll be right down," David said without knowing for sure that it was true.

"Thanks."

David didn't bother with social amenities like casual conversation. He pretended to busy himself with the tree.

"Good job with the lights," Ted said. "You hung them the same way your dad always did."

David stepped back from the tree. "I didn't know Dad had a particular 'way' with the Christmas lights."

"The flashing ones on the inside, closest to the trunk, and the solid ones on the outside," Ted explained. "He didn't like the flashing ones on the outside. He said it made the tree look like police cars at a car accident."

David folded his arms and grunted.

After a moment, Ted asked him if there was anything hot to drink.

"Like what?" David asked.

Ted eyed him for a moment, then said, "I'll find something if you don't mind. I know where everything is."

David shrugged.

Ted had just finished making himself some hot chocolate and had walked back into the living room when Ruth came down the stairs in a bathrobe, my wife's oversized pink slippers, and her hair up in a towel. She was saying, "Why did you call me? Is something wrong?"

Then she saw Ted. She shrieked.

"Hiya," he said.

She turned crimson. "What are you doing here?" She spun and glared at her brother. "Why didn't you say we had a guest?"

"It's only Ted," David said without looking up from the tree.

She made a low growling noise, then said to Ted, "I'll be back in a minute."

David smirked. Ted smiled.

Five minutes later she returned, her hair still wet but pulled back. She had traded the bathrobe and slippers for jeans, a flannel shirt, and thick hiking socks. She went up to Ted and gave him a quick hug. "Hi," she said.

David looked at them both, smirk still in place. He went to the door, slipped into his overcoat, and announced that he was going out for awhile.

He was gone before Ruth could ask where he was planning to go.

Alone with Ted now, Ruth asked, "So what are you doing here?"

"I was in the area. Sledding with some kids over by Chimney Hill." Ted went over to his coat and produced a green scarf from an inside pocket. "I think you left this at my shop. I'm returning it to you."

Ruth glanced at the scarf. "It's not mine."

"It isn't?" Ted asked. Undaunted, he thrust the scarf into her hands. "Well, then, Merry Christmas."

"What?"

"It's a gift," he said. He walked over to the small fireplace.

"But—" She noticed the price tag was still on the scarf and giggled. It was a sound I hadn't heard from her in a long time.

"On a night like this..." He put kindling into the grate and began to arrange the logs for a fire.

She wrapped the scarf around her neck and joined him in front of the hearth. She reached up and found the long matches in the box on the mantle. The fire was lit and soon began to burn in earnest.

Ted gestured to the tree. "You haven't gotten very far with this tree," he said.

Ruth stepped over to the neglected Scotch pine. "I left David to do it. But he wasn't very interested."

"He looks fairly miserable," Ted observed.

"I think my family is headed for a nervous breakdown," Ruth said.

"Really?" Ted asked as he picked up a gold Christmas ball and hooked it to a limb on the tree.

Ruth grabbed another ornament and hung it on the other side. "Why can't we mourn like other families? Why can't we just hug each other and cry like normal people? I've got a depressed artist upstairs who can't finish a painting—and an obsessed brother who can't balance my dad's checkbook—and I—" She was suddenly aware that he was looking at her. "I have to finish this tree."

"Finish what you were going to say," Ted said gently. When she didn't speak, he prodded her. "What's happening to *you*, Ruth?"

"Nothing."

"I'm sorry about what I said at the shop," Ted said. "I had no right to be so opinionated."

"Forget it," she replied.

Ted fiddled with a few more ornaments. "I have a confession to make. I saw you after you left the shop—"

Ruth glanced at him suspiciously. "Were you stalking me?"

He said quickly, "It's a small town, and I decided to take the afternoon off. You were walking down the street with a bunch of shopping bags in your arms. Your cheeks were all red from the cold and everybody was talking to you."

"You *are* stalking me."

"I was *looking* for you. Two different things. My probation officer will attest to it."

Ruth giggled again.

"But when I found you, I realized it'd be better not to bother you. I didn't want to spoil your day by making you mad at me twice."

Ruth gazed at Ted silently.

"You didn't look tired," Ted said as if that was his whole point. "You looked healthy and alive."

"It was a brisk, invigorating day."

"It's not just the day," Ted said. "Admit it. You like being here."

"It has its moments."

He turned from the tree to face her. "What would it take to . . ." He shuffled nervously. "To get you to come back home, Ruth?"

Ruth countered his position by moving around the tree, ostensibly to put another ornament there.

"You don't want to talk about it," Ted said.

"Not really."

"Why not? It's a simple question. It doesn't commit you to anything."

"I told you."

"I don't believe the big city/small town case you made before. There's something else. What is it?"

Ruth shrugged from her side of the tree.

"If you gestured as an answer, I couldn't see it from here," Ted said.

She smiled. "I shrugged."

Ted moved around to her side of the tree. "You don't know what's wrong?"

She looked at him but didn't answer.

"Look, I know you're a proud woman and—"

She held up a hand. "Proud?"

"You're worried about what people will think," he clarified.

"Why should I care what they think?"

Ted tilted his head and gave her a sideways glance, a wry smile. "Why *do* you care what they think?"

"I don't," she said without conviction.

"You do. I know you do. Maybe you can fool some of the folks around here, but you can't fool me. I know you too well."

"What makes you think I care?" She turned away from him and went to my small stereo tucked into the bookcase. She pretended to look for something to play—Elvis had finished a while ago. Ruth settled for an old Firestone Christmas album with singers like Julie Andrews, Robert Goulet, and the Mormon Tabernacle Choir. She hit the play button. "Silent Night" began.

"What do you want from me, Ted? I came to bury my father. Don't you think that's enough of a major life change for the moment?" Ruth asked. "What do you want? Why are you *really* here?"

Ted contemplated her for a moment, then said: "I love you, Ruth. I never stopped loving you."

Surprised, she turned away.

Ted continued, "This isn't just a small-town boy with a crush. I know what love is. And I know that I love you."

"You don't know what you're saying, Ted," Ruth said without looking at him. "You can't love me. You don't even know me. You know the old Ruth, the Ruth I used to be, the small-town, simple-and-true Ruth. I've changed. I've been through some things... done some things..."

"Old Ruth, New Ruth. I don't care. You're Ruth," Ted affirmed. "I love *you*—whoever you were, whoever you are."

"Nobody loves like that."

"You're wrong, and you know it." Ted's gaze went over to the crucifix hanging by the door. "There is a love like that. What do you think Christmas is all about?"

She followed his gaze, glanced at the crucifix, and didn't answer.

"Maybe we can't love the way *he* loves, but we can do our best." Ted took a step towards her.

"You don't get it," Ruth began, and stopped.

"What don't I get?" he asked. "Let me guess. For some reason you think you've been a terrible person. You think you've done things that people in a town like this couldn't possibly understand or forgive. Or maybe you're thinking of your dad. I don't know. Maybe you have done things we can't understand. But *I* understand that I love you no matter what you've done." He locked his gaze on her. "There. I said it."

She dropped down onto the couch, her head lowered. Then she looked up at him with a steely expression, harder than anything I've ever seen on her. "Would you say all of this if you knew I was *pregnant*? Would you? Would my dad?"

Then the facade broke and the tears came in a torrent. Hers and mine.

Now I understood her pain. It washed over me like lava. Worse, I understood why she was so conflicted. In this moment I wanted to reach out to her, take her in my arms, and do all I could to comfort her. I couldn't. I looked to Ted.

He sat down next to her and took her hand in his as she wept. Then he pulled her close for a long embrace.

"The answer is 'yes.'"

"You're saying that because you think you should. It's not that easy," she said between sobs.

"It isn't easy. I've had all day to think about it," Ted said. "I knew this morning."

Ruth pulled away from him. "How can you know that?"

"Before you left the shop, your purse fell..." he said calmly. "When we put everything back in I saw a brochure for a clinic, somewhere in LA. You'd written a date and time on it."

She looked at him, dumbfounded.

There were so many things I wanted to say then. More than anything, I wanted to beg her not to go through with it. No matter how bleak her situation seemed to be, she didn't have to go through with it. No voice of my own, I prayed for Ted to say the right thing.

"I know what you want," he said softly to her. "The same thing the rest of us want. A clean slate. You want forgiveness."

She closed her eyes and shook her head.

"You know where to find it." Ted said it so quietly that I wasn't sure she heard him.

But Ruth slowly nodded. The tears came again.

Chapter Eight

CARMICHAEL'S WAS a ramshackle building with no windows, dented aluminum siding, a wide front door with a diamond-shaped window in the middle, and a half-lit sign that said *C rm cha l's*. It had started off forty years ago as a tavern that later proclaimed itself as a bar, then a lounge, then a pub, then a sports bar (after Billy Carmichael replaced the nineteen-inch TV above the bar with a thirty-five incher), and was now considered merely a shack by most of us who lived within walking distance of it.

Kathryn and I went there occasionally because Billy Carmichael had an even more extensive collection of Elvis paraphernalia than we did. He'd won an award from the National Elvis Fan Club for building a duplicate of Graceland out of sugar cubes. That made the network news, too. A month or so later a problem with the sprinkler system put an end to that.

David sat sour-faced at the far end of the horseshoe-shaped bar, next to the cheaply paneled wall, under the gaze of a buxom blonde on a large poster advertising a beer. He hunched over the bar as if it had been his favorite haunt for years, in spite of the odd looks he kept getting from the other patrons. His expensive coat and finely tailored clothes made him an odd site among the plaid jackets and worn hunting coats. He drank what I thought was a coke, but then I noticed when he asked for another refill that it was Jack Daniels.

"That's the last one," Mickey the bartender said with a sharp look of disapproval.

"You don't tell me how many drinks I can have," David insisted, his voice thick from too many drinks. "It's a free country."

"Free country, not a free bar," someone said with a laugh nearby. I think it was Walter Irving, owner of Irving's Towing Service.

"*Last* drink," Mickey said firmly. "So make it last."

David reached into his pocket and pulled out a wad of bills. He slapped a twenty onto the bar. "There."

Mickey took the twenty, then said: "I'll use this to call you a cab."

David frowned. "What's your problem anyway?" He slurred so that it sounded more like "Whatsyurprobumanyway?"

Mickey leaned on the bar. "Your father's funeral Mass is tomorrow, isn't it?"

"Yeah—so what?"

"So, I think it's a shame the son of Richard Lee would be such an ass," Mickey said. Mickey was always a good kid. I taught him Sunday School when he was in eighth grade.

A large, heavy-set man I didn't recognize slid—if *slid* is the right word for the movement—over a couple of stools and took a good look at David. "You're Richard Lee's boy?" he asked with a worse slur than David's.

"Yeah."

The man clapped him on the back just as David was about to drink. Half the contents of the glass went down the front of his clothes. "Hey!"

"I liked your father," the man said, his jowls shaking merrily. "He was a good man. Gave me a job when I needed one."

"What did you do for him?"

"I cleaned his office. When he had one in the old Palmer building."

Oz Trent. He'd put on a lot of weight since I'd last seen him.

"Good for you," David said.

"He was a good man."

"Yeah, yeah, he was a good man," David nodded, unconvinced.

Oz took a closer look at David. "You're the oldest, right? Donald."

"David."

"That's what I said. You're the one who did so well making money, right? Or are you the house painter?"

"Look, I'd really like to—"

"You must be the whiz-kid with the money." Oz tugged at David's coat as if to confirm it, then shook his head sadly. "Your father was proud of you kids. You and the house painter and—you had a sister, right? He talked about you all the time." Since I hadn't seen Oz in several years, I couldn't imagine how he knew I had talked about my children. Then again, maybe I talked about them more than I realized.

David looked at Oz, mildly surprised.

Oz drew his mug of beer to his lips. "He had a picture of you in his office—you on a horse. Did you ever own a horse?"

"No?"

"You were on something. I don't remember. But I cleaned that picture when I cleaned the office. You were a cute kid." Then he remembered. "You were on a bike."

David brooded as he remembered the bike. I'd bought it second-hand. It hadn't met up with his expectations any more than the car with the pedals.

"What the heck are you doing in this place? You don't belong in here," Oz finally said after a long pause.

"Not good enough for me?" David asked with a snarl. "I'm sure it was good enough for my father. I'll bet he bought all the rounds."

Carter Smith slammed his glass down on the other side of the bar. "Okay, that's it. I think we need to have a chat."

Carter used to be a regular at our church until his real estate business took off four or five years ago. He brokered a deal to bring a large internet company to town, along with their seven hundred employees. Carter worked around the clock trying to sell houses to maximize on the "boom." His fortunes rose, and he became our local success story. He and his family lived the high life. But fortune can be fickle, and, a year ago, the company was bought out by a competitor and quickly closed down. Suddenly Hope Springs wasn't the "location, location, location" that Carter so urgently needed it to be. His heavy investment into the *Quail Run* development behind my house didn't pay off. They had hoped for well-to-do upwardly mobile buyers to pay exorbitant prices for their cardboard boxes. Instead, the upwardly mobile went to the outskirts of Denver and the houses at *Quail Run* were sold at rock-bottom prices to people who used to live in the trailer parks. Last I'd heard Carter's business was on the verge of bankruptcy, and he'd been drinking more than he'd been working.

David squinted at Carter. "What did you say?"

Carter, a large barrel-chested man, pushed off of his stool and spoke as he rounded the bar towards my son. "I said, I think we need to have a chat."

"What kind of bar is this?" David asked Mickey. "I just wanted a quiet drink."

"*Several* quiet drinks," Mickey observed.

"I've been sitting over there for the past hour trying to figure you out," Carter said.

"Nothing interesting on the TV?" David asked.

"I've got a satellite dish," Mickey said.

"Where does all this dripping sarcasm come from?" Carter asked.

"My sarcasm?"

"Are you going to answer all my questions with questions?"

"I don't know—am I?"

"You're Richard's boy and yet you come in here with an attitude. You make snide remarks about us, about him—and I don't get it. What's your problem?"

"You're the one with the problem." David hung his head over his drink. "He's *my* father, and I can say whatever I want about him."

"Not in here you can't. Your father deserves *respect*. He was a—"

"Good man," David finished the sentence. "I know."

Carter poked a hard finger into David's shoulder. "Don't toy with me, son."

David spread his arms as if in submission. "Toying with you? I'm not toying with you."

Carter waved at Mickey for another of whatever he was drinking. He sat down next to David. David looked affronted.

"Nice suit," Carter said. "Must've set you back a bundle."

"I've got connections. I only pay a few dollars over cost."

Carter grunted. "You probably get good deals on a lot of things. You're shrewd with your money."

"I don't like to *waste it*, if that's what you mean."

"I get it." Carter smiled as he leaned into his drink.

"Get what?" David looked confused. "Are you still talking to me or did someone else come in on this conversation?"

"It's as clear as the nose on your face," Carter said.

David nearly reached up to touch his nose. "What is?"

Carter leaned forward and whispered in a thick, alcohol-saturated voice, "Look, kid, we're not so different. I know what's going on."

David teased him with a mock conspiratorial whisper, "Really? What do you think is going on?"

"You think that just because you left town and made a lot of money that you're better than people like us, people like your father."

"Is that what I think?"

"You betcha. Well, let me tell you something..." He looked around as if making sure that no one was eavesdropping. Everyone was, but he continued anyway. "In my best year, I've spent more on tips than you'll make in a decade. Do you hear me?"

"You don't know how much I make."

"I know all about raking in the cash. I've been there. I know."

"Good for you."

"And I also know a thing or two about respecting people. But let me tell you something..."

David closed his eyes, as if waiting for the pain. "Do I have a choice?"

Carter leaned closer. "Making money and respecting people don't always go hand-in-hand. Are you with me?"

David opened his eyes. "No."

"Just because you're rolling in the dough doesn't mean you're the cat's meow."

David looked at him, perplexed. "Is that a mixed metaphor?"

"What's bull-fighting got to do with this?"

"*Metaphor* not *matador*."

Carter ignored the correction and poked him in the shoulder again, his voice rising. "What you've got in your wallet is nothing compared to what you've got inside. That's what I'm saying. It's who you are in *here*—" he poked at David's chest "—that counts. And your daddy had a lot in there."

"That's right!" Jason Finch said, raising a glass from a table behind them. "He bailed me out when the bank tried to evict me a couple of years ago!"

"*More* money he gave away," David muttered.

"He gave it away, and he helped people, and he never seemed to think of himself. Isn't that right?" Carter asked whoever happened to be listening.

"That's right!" a few shouted in reply.

Carter spoke like a tent-revival, Bible-thumping Baptist.

David looked at Carter expectantly. But Carter fell quiet, as if he'd said all he had to say. Then he said suddenly, "I think it's time to go." He dropped off the stool and staggered away.

None of this helped David's mood. He struggled off of his barstool, endured a vigorous farewell handshake from Oz, and made his way to the door.

Mickey was on the phone. "I've got a cab coming for you."

"I'm walking home," David announced. "You can keep that twenty. Consider it another *donation* from my family."

It was supposed to be a final rebuke and a strong exit line, except David marched into the ladies room instead of marching out the front door as he'd planned. The patrons of Carmichael's applauded when he emerged, red-faced. He stumbled out the correct door.

"I'm almost positive he was adopted," Oz said and drained the last of his beer.

I watched David stumble home, and his drunken state told me two things. One, he obviously didn't drink very often. Two, he should drink even less, because he made a silly-looking drunk. The alcohol had loosened him up considerably. He began to softly sing "Rudolph the Red-Nosed Reindeer" and got lost in the names of the reindeer, winding up with Frosty the Snowman and Peter Cottontail. By the time he reached the line "used to laugh and call him names," he was singing loudly.

Mrs. Fitzgerald, who was always ready to squash any disturbance in the neighborhood, turned on her porch light, stepped out, and threatened to call the police if he didn't shut up. David told her to go back inside, or he'd have her committed.

He stumbled onward. The frozen snow crunched under the soles of his shoes. At one point he stopped and looked down. "It sounds like I'm eating a bowl of Captain Crunch," he said.

He tripped going up the three steps to the front porch and collided with the front door. After a minute or two of negotiation, he got it open and walked into the living room, which was lit only by the reds, greens, yellows, and blues of the Christmas tree. Ruth and Ted had been busy while we were gone. The tinsel and ornaments sparkled and shone like a soft-focus picture.

Attracted by the glow, David went to the tree and stared at it for a moment. There was no guessing what his blurry-eyes saw there. Slowly he got down on his knees, like a child ready to open a Christmas present, and stared at the flashing bulbs.

His face had an expression of awe I hadn't seen in years.

Jonathan walked in from the kitchen carrying a glass of milk. He was wearing my old robe. "What in the world?" He turned on a light.

David spun around and shrieked as if he'd seen a ghost.

Jonathan nearly dropped his glass of milk. "David!"

David pointed accusingly. "You're wearing Dad's robe! How dare you wear his robe?"

"I forgot mine."

"You can't wear that robe! It was a gift from *me*."

Jonathan walked closer to his brother. "You've been drinking."

"No, I haven't," David argued. "I've been *drinking*."

"My mistake."

"It's Christmas. The reason for the season!" he announced, then added as a matter of full-disclosure: "I read that on a button somewhere."

Jonathan cocked an eyebrow. "Uh huh."

"What are you doing down here? Why aren't you working on your painting? Did you finish it?"

"Nope," Jonathan replied. "And it won't be finished." He sipped his milk casually.

David clumsily pulled himself to his feet. "Figures," he said. "I knew you wouldn't finish it. You can't finish anything you start."

"Don't start," Jonathan said.

"That's why they threw you out of that art school in San Francisco. You couldn't finish anything."

Jonathan glared at his brother, then headed for the staircase. "I'm going to bed."

"Tell me what you know about the Foster Fund."

"The *Foster*—?" Jonathan frowned. "Are you back on that again?"

"Back? I never left it."

"I've never heard of the thing."

"Why should I believe you?"

Jonathan shook his head. "You're bad enough sober. You're even worse when you're drunk. I have nothing to say to you." Jonathan turned away.

"Don't you walk away from me!" David shouted, putting on what he thought was a threatening expression. It looked more like he was breaking wind.

Jonathan faced him again, his gaze cold. "Why are you so obsessed about it?"

"Why aren't *you* obsessed about it?" David asked. "Our father, who couldn't even afford to put us through school, gave his money away to that stupid fund. Money we should have had. Doesn't that bug you? Because it sure bugs me. Just like that stupid little car bugs me about everything that bugs me about me."

Jonathan leaned forward as if he'd misheard David. "What did you say?"

David looked confused as he leaned against the wall. He rubbed his face with his hands. "This doesn't make sense. I was *happy* with my life until now. I have everything that Dad *didn't* have. Do you know what Dad has? This lousy house in this lousy town and a lousy life insurance policy that no self-respecting dead person would admit to having. He has no value. I don't want to die like that."

Jonathan put his glass of milk down on the end table and said, "Stand up straight for a minute."

"Huh?"

"Stand up straight."

With some effort, David pushed away from the wall and stood up straight, as if he thought Jonathan was going to straighten his collar or adjust a button.

"Thanks," Jonathan said. Then punched David in the jaw. It wasn't a hard punch. Not enough to do any real damage. But David spun as if he'd been clobbered by a fist of anvil and fell hard to the floor.

Jonathan stood over him and said through clenched teeth, "Don't ever talk about Dad like that. Don't *ever* reduce him to your pathetic little dollar signs and portfolios and decimal points on a spreadsheet. You may think you're a success, but you'll never be the man that Dad was. No matter what you say or how much money you make, you'll never be the man he was."

Jonathan walked back over to the end table, picked up his glass of milk, and walked up the stairs.

David lay sprawled on the floor, working his jaw. "Yeah. I know," he said to the empty room.

Chapter Nine

THOUGH I now feel a sense of peace and clarity of mind in my current state, I am not stoic. I'm feeling emotions in ways I never felt them when I was alive. I can't account for it, but death has somehow made me feel more alive.

From where I sit—or stand—or whatever my bodiless position might be, I am embarrassed and humbled by the comments made about me by the folks at Carmichael's. Jonathan's loyalty touches me deeply, as well. But I do not see myself now as they remember me. I know that I was not always as selfless as I should have been. Sometimes I helped others as a matter of generosity, sometimes as a matter of duty, often as a matter of instinct. My motives were not always pure. I never thought that they had to be. It was enough to take action, to do *something*, to do *anything*. Helping became a default position. It was simply the Christian thing to do.

It never occurred to me that helping others would drive a wedge between me and my oldest son. Just the opposite: I thought I was being a good example to him, to all three of my kids. But now, on the morning of my funeral, I could see my three children struggling with their feelings about me.

David stood at the mirror in his room, working and reworking his Italian silk tie. His mind wasn't on it. His head throbbed and his jaw was bruised and tender for a reason he couldn't remember clearly. Had he fallen? Did someone at the bar hit him in the jaw?

He thought of Oz and, somewhere in the fuzziness of his memory, he also saw my office when it was in the Palmer building downtown and then came an image—the picture of his younger self on the second-hand bike. We'd given him that bike for his twelfth birthday and by that time his attitude—possibly aroused by the Christmas car incident—was set on its course. He hated that bike because I'd bought it a garage sale. But seeds of doubt now fell into the soggy soil of his hungover mind.

There was nothing wrong with the bike. In some ways it was probably as good, if not better, than a new bike at twice the price. Maybe he was wrong.

He thought of Carter. He knew Carter had been a success financially but was now in deep trouble; a man who now regularly drank to excess most nights.

His sober self wondered if Carter was a glimpse into his own future—a sort of ghost of Christmas yet-to-come—if he didn't get rid of his obsession about all he felt he'd been denied by me.

Then he remembered Jonathan. It came back to him like a movie fade-in. Jonathan had slugged him after he came back from Carmichael's. He couldn't recall the specifics but had a vague notion he deserved it.

A long exhale and David adjusted his tie, looking at himself in the mirror.

I prayed that he would continue his line of thought. He was onto something important, maybe life-changing. But his defenses were strong. The Foster Fund came back to mind. If the little pedal-car had been a symbol of my denial of his wants, the Foster Fund had become a symbol of my denial of his needs. It was flagrant neglect. I had robbed from him to give to others—and he was going to get to the bottom of it. The Foster Fund would give him an important piece to the puzzle—the piece that would answer his questions about my life, and his.

In the attic, Jonathan stood fully dressed in an old black suit. He stared at his half-finished painting. The concept was in place: people from all walks of life, all nations, surrounded the Nativity, looking in adoration. Everyone—including Mary, Joseph, the shepherds, and the Wise Men were rendered and partially painted. I was never an artist, but what he'd done looked glorious to me.

The glaring problem, the big obstacle, was the face of the Christ child. It wasn't there. Not even as a rough outline.

I wondered impatiently why he couldn't simply put in the face of any baby. Use the Gerber baby's face. It wouldn't matter to anyone, as long as it was respectful and cute.

But it mattered to Jonathan. He didn't want just any face for the baby. He wanted a face that came from his own imagination, his own heart. And he couldn't *see* it.

Shoving his hands in his suit-coat pockets, he began to pace angrily. "Why can't I do it? Why can't I finish the child?" he asked in lamentation.

He dropped the cover over the painting and, in a decisive move, took the canvas off of the easel and placed it with a certain finality against the wall.

Ruth nervously tidied up the living room, alternately crying for me and singing "I'll Be Home for Christmas," that melancholy World War II wish. It took on an entirely different meaning for her now. Eventually she collapsed into my easy chair and said, "This is a miserable way to spend Christmas."

Never in my wildest dreams would I have thought I'd be buried during Advent or Christmas—or any other major holiday season, for that matter. But, then again, who tries to imagine on what day in the year he will die or be buried? Still, if I had my choice, it wouldn't have been during Advent.

My mind ticked through what little I knew about the Catholic Church's rules for funerals. I vaguely remembered that Sundays were a no-go for funerals during Church seasons like Advent and Lent, or on Holy Days of Obligation. David and Father Cliff must have decided to have the funeral Mass on the Saturday before Christmas rather than wait until, say, a day after Christmas. David's motive was probably to get the funeral over with as soon as possible so he could quickly escape from town. Waiting another few days would have been maddening for him.

My only hope, if I could have one, was that it would be a proper funeral Mass, but that the tone wouldn't be unduly sad.

It turned out to be an interesting mix. A makeshift choir sang my favorite hymns, selected by Jonathan and Ruth. Fortunately, my taste in hymns leaned toward the hopeful and eternal. Father Cliff's homily reminded the congregation of two things that he was sure I'd tell them if I could speak from the grave. (I couldn't wait to hear this.) First, life is fleeting and death comes upon us so unexpectedly. Second, we must be spiritually prepared for the day when we shuffle off our mortal coils. He spoke, then, of living lives of faith through Jesus, who was and is the Resurrection and the Life. Father Cliff closed by reiterating that death was not the end of a process begun at birth, but the beginning of a truer birth—much as Christ was born, not just to die, but to rise again.

My coffin, placed at the foot of the altar, was draped with a purple cloth. Fortunately, for me, the lid was closed. I don't know how I would have felt looking at my dead self. Corpses, I've always found, were hardly ever good representations of the living. If nothing else, the hair is never quite right. And the face is little more than a wax museum likeness. And I couldn't remember if I'd shaved that morning or not.

I noticed that David, Jonathan, and Ruth did not go forward to receive the Eucharist.

Before the final blessing, Father Cliff announced that we would have the interment at the cemetery, which was only a stone's throw from the church, then there would be a reception in the church hall.

More snow had fallen during the Mass, making the cemetery a pristine white. I watched the crowd huddle in the cold as the coffin descended into the rectangular grave. Even there, Father Cliff spoke positively about the coffin and its contents being more than mere vessels, though now devoid of the soul of the real Richard Lee. He spoke of the great hope of the real Richard Lee being united with God in Heaven—and there was no better place to be.

Was I with God? I suppose so, since God is everywhere, but I still hadn't solved the mystery of where I was and how I was able to see these scenes. But watching the coffin disappear into a hole next to my wife's grave filled me with an emotion I hardly know how to describe. Melancholy, perhaps, but not hopelessness; sad, but not despairing. I'm sure the French have a word for it.

I wondered if, somehow, my wife would appear at my side. She didn't.

The reception in the church hall offered tables laden with copious amounts of food, compliments of the parish ladies' committee. Huge helpings of chicken casseroles, pot roasts, sliced ham, potato salad, corn on the cob, sweet peas, baked beans, Vienna sausages in a tangy barbecue sauce, and homemade bread were dished out onto paper plates with plastic cutlery from the church kitchen.

A podium was set up for people to say a few words about me. I dreaded it.

Chuck Crosby, a deacon who'd served the church for years, told some amusing stories about my days on the parish council, highlighting the meeting where I'd fallen asleep during one discussion and knocked a jug of water off the table.

Joel Lewis remembered the time I was an usher and had been asked by Father to put extra batteries in my pocket for his wireless microphone. Unfortunately, I put the batteries in the same pocket as my loose change—and my trousers caught fire.

Kevin Ladd told comical stories about my brief stint as coach of the young people's softball team. During one practice, I'd stood too close to the batter and got hit in the family jewels by his back swing.

Margaret Simpson recalled the first and only time Kathryn and I tried to play golf—and I was nearly struck by lightning during the attempt. Fortunately, a nearby tree took the biggest hit. But my hair stood on end for the rest of the day.

I laughed at the memory of my singed hair and eyebrows, the way my belt buckle had shot off and my trousers nearly dropped, and the burn I received around my wedding ring.

I never took lightning storms for granted again.

Our new mayor, Jeff Cassidy, had a word or two to say about my philanthropic efforts in our town. Then Ruth stood up as the representative of the family, said a few words of thanks, then wept with such heavy sobs that Jonathan had to escort her back to her chair. Father Cliff recovered the moment by talking about my love of family and of the people in the town and of life in general. He reminisced about our arguments over the rise and fall of Elvis and who was better: the Beatles or the Rolling Stones.

Ted Hagan stepped up and, teary-eyed, lavished undue praise on me. Had I been there, I would have told him to sit down. But I wasn't. He eventually finished by announcing that I was the inspiration for his new bookshop and café and that I had generously helped get it started.

David's sour expression didn't surprise me.

The testimonials ended and, all in all, I was relieved. Nothing was said that sounded insincere or gratuitous. It felt as it was: a group of people remembering an old friend.

Then, unexpectedly, Nancy Daugherty, a woman who deluded herself as being a poet, stood up and read a tribute to me that she'd written the night before. The first few lines were a good effort, if one enjoyed hackneyed rhymes and a Victorian sensibility with its sentimental view of death and a propensity towards cherubs and winged chariots. A few older ladies in the crowd were moved and wept openly. That would have been all right. But Nancy always had a habit of writing poems of epic proportions with what I called "trick stanzas." Those were stanzas that sounded as if the poem was about to finish, and then it didn't. Nancy's poetry was like singing a round of "Row, Row, Row Your Boat"—you simply never knew if and when it would ever end.

It eventually finished, and she sat down, smiling modestly to no applause, touching lightly her loose strands of metal-like hair and checking her lace collar.

The event was done. Ruth and Father Cliff passed the word to some of the attendees about coffee back at my house. It would be a much smaller group of closer friends, it seemed.

David, Jonathan, and Ruth arrived sooner than everyone else. Jonathan decided to get out of the suit and into something more comfortable. David tugged at his tie. Ruth checked her black dress for wrinkles. She took a cloth to smudges of makeup on her shoulder, left by women who hugged close enough to lose a layer or two.

David stood at the Christmas tree and seemed to meditate upon the lights.

"Are you okay?" Ruth asked him.

"Just dandy," he said with the expression of a man who needed some industrial-strength Alka-Seltzer. He moved from the tree to the sliding glass door that overlooked my back yard and the path to the pond.

"It was a nice funeral Mass, wasn't it?"

"As funeral Masses go, I think so."

"It had the right tone."

David turned to her. "Tone?"

"The Mass, the reception," she explained. "It felt like an appropriate celebration of Dad. I kept thinking he would suddenly appear to take a bow. I've never been to a funeral like it."

David shrugged. "Maybe it's because of Christmas."

"Or maybe it's because of something else," she said thoughtfully.

David looked at her.

"It's something Ted reminded me about last night. About what we were raised to believe." She looked at David nervously. "I think I've always believed various things because I was supposed to, but now..." She struggled for the words, fiddling with the cuff of her sleeve. "Mom and Dad's faith—and Ted's—is *real.* It's..."

"Simple?"

"Innocent. True."

David didn't say anything.

She continued, "I get so jaded and cynical that I want to dismiss it—even laugh at it. My cynicism wants to snuff it out, because that's what cynicism does." She fiddled with her other cuff.

David kept his silence.

"I don't want to be cynical anymore," she said and looked up at him. "I want... to feel the way I used to."

David turned to look out at the back yard again.

"Does that make sense?" Ruth asked.

He half-smiled. "Not at all."

But it did. I knew that he knew what she was talking about.

She looked away self-consciously and softly said, "I want to have faith again." It was like a child's wish.

Before she could say anything else, voices and banging feet on the porch announced the arrival of the guests.

David sighed. "Here we go."

Ruth gave him a sympathetic look and went to the door.

It looked as if everyone who'd attended the funeral service decided they couldn't pass up coffee at our house. Mary Bergman, the ever-efficient secretary at St. Clare's, took over as barista. Father

Cliff directed the rest as they all crammed into the house. Food from the reception was placed on the counters and tables. Bottles of wine were opened. And, mysteriously, bottles of Jameson's and Dalmore and Crown Royal appeared.

Ted Hagan helped serve the drinks, but I noticed that he kept an eye on Ruth no matter where she was.

The mood was upbeat and I caught bits of conversations as more people remembered things that Kathryn and I had done in Hope Springs. I was pleased to hear them talk about Kathryn, feeling as I did that she'd been left out until now.

I don't know when it happened, but Ruth had changed out of her mourning dress and was now wearing jeans and a sweater. Jonathan wore one of my flannel shirts. David stood off to the side in his sharp suit looking uncomfortable.

Occasionally, someone remembered an embarrassing story about the kids: when Jonathan got stuck on a neighbor's roof after chasing a wild Frisbee, and when Ruth got into a rock-throwing contest with Wendy Phipps and needed seven stitches in her head. And there was the time David went to the Walkers' house and fell down their laundry chute, a full three floors, and into a large clothes hamper at the bottom.

The laughter was good—and right—and I was grateful to hear it in my house again.

David was not amused. In fact, he wasn't amused by anything about the affair. I watched as his initial discomfort turned into irritation and then anger. He seethed as the gathering turned into a full-fledged party.

Horace Hecht sat down at our old Kendall piano and encouraged everyone to sing a few of my favorite Christmas songs. Horace was always a well-meaning but stiff traditionalist, so I couldn't have been happier when he suddenly launched into his own version of "Blue Christmas." It was the perfect icebreaker and soon everyone was singing along, complete with those awful back-up vocals.

The final verse approached and Horace, noticing how uninvolved David had been, shouted out for him to "take it!"

David merely glared at him.

Horace played on and looked at him helplessly. "David?"

David suddenly pushed through the crowd and stormed to the sliding glass door.

"David!" Ruth called out, annoyed. The music stopped, the room went silent, as all eyes turned to my oldest son.

David stood at the sliding glass door with his back to the room. His shoulders moved as if the tension was a living force that worked through the muscles there. He then spun around to face the crowd. "What's wrong with you people? My *father* is dead! Why don't you go home and sing your ridiculous Christmas songs there?"

This time there was no exit, except to push through the crowd again. Instead he yanked the sliding glass door open and marched outside into the cold winter afternoon.

Backing towards the door, Ruth gestured with embarrassment. "No, don't go. It's all right. He didn't mean it. Tell them, Jonathan." She followed David out the door.

Jonathan smiled sheepishly. "Don't mind my brother. He's only in need of a personality transplant." Jonathan also slipped out the back door.

Somebody said, "You know, I heard he was adopted."

Horace hit the keys again for "Hark! The Herald Angels Sing."

"David!" Ruth shouted, barely keeping up with him as he stomped through the snow. He was headed to the pond. "What's the matter with you?"

He suddenly stopped. "What's the matter with all of *you*? We buried our father today, and you're acting like you're at an office Christmas party."

"Is that the problem?" she asked breathlessly. It was cold.

He grunted and turned, continued onward.

"That's not the problem," she called after him, keeping pace. "It's cold out here! Are you having a nervous breakdown?"

Jonathan caught up with them both. "Nice exit. You should have studied drama instead of finance."

David didn't respond. He followed the path as Ruth followed him as Jonathan followed her. They reached the pond. The dim sunlight through the overcast sky gave it the washed-out quality of an old photo.

I glanced at the rock where I had slipped and felt embarrassed. Heart attack or no heart attack, it still seemed like a silly way to go.

"Why are you burying it, David?" Ruth folded her arms, pressing them close.

"Don't patronize me with your pop-psychoanalysis."

"You didn't cry at the funeral, you haven't cried all week," she persisted. "Why don't you let it go?"

"Where and when I cry is *my* business," he snapped and paced at the edge of the pond aimlessly.

"Then why make a scene?" Jonathan asked. "Couldn't you just slip away quietly?"

"It made me angry, turning Dad's funeral into some kind of festival."

"Don't you think that's what he would've wanted?" asked Ruth.

"I have no idea what he would've wanted," David said sharply. "Look, I just want to settle the estate, sell the house, and get out of here."

"Sell the house!" Ruth said. "Who said we're selling the house?" She turned to Jonathan. "Did you know?"

Jonathan shrugged. "He mentioned it."

"What if I don't want to sell the house?" she challenged them.

David groaned. "We have to sell the house. *I* don't want to play landlord. Do either of you?"

"Can we talk about this where it isn't so cold?" Jonathan asked.

David ignored him. "Unless one of you wants to move in, it has to be sold."

"No," Ruth said firmly. "It's part of the family. I can't stand the thought of it going to strangers."

"Are *you* willing to move in?" he asked.

She frowned at him but didn't answer.

"There. You want to keep it, but you don't want the responsibility of it," David said. He kicked at a clump of snow, then muttered, "Typical."

Father Cliff rounded the corner of the path. Merciful and smart man that he was, he carried coats for David, Jonathan, and Ruth. Following him was a man dressed almost as nicely as David, wearing an overcoat that spoke of good taste in clothes. He had a full head of wavy, perfectly cut, silver hair and looked like the kind of man whose age was making him a better person. Even his walk spoke of training and integrity. I was surprised to see him. And I knew why he'd come.

"What now?" David murmured. "Is he here to lead us in party games? Maybe some pin-the-tail-on-the-donkey?"

"Easy to guess which part you'd play," Jonathan said.

"No point to your freezing out here." Father Cliff handed out the coats and then gestured to the stranger. "This is Kenneth Walsh, an old friend of your father's and mine. He lives in Denver."

Mr. Walsh smiled. "You don't know me. But, then again, there's no reason you should. But I know you. Your mother and father talked about you all the time."

The three of them watched him in silence.

Walsh directed his gaze to David. "I'm the administrator of the Foster Fund, David."

"Oh, really?" David's eyes went sharp. "I hope you've come with a few answers."

"The Foster Fund?" Ruth asked.

"If you'd like to go back inside—or somewhere else—we can talk about it." Kenneth's deep baritone was calm, the voice of warmth and comfort.

"This is as good a place as any," David said. He put on his gloves, like a man preparing for a fight.

"What's going on here?" Ruth asked Father Cliff.

Father Cliff inclined his head towards David and Kenneth.

"Tell me about that fund. What is it? Where did my dad's money go?" He eyed the stranger from head to toe. His expression implied that Kenneth's nice coat, his clothes, even his immaculate haircut was paid for by my money.

"A lot of different things," Kenneth said. He gestured toward the house again as an invitation to move back inside. "Are you sure you wouldn't rather go someplace warm?"

David didn't budge. "What are you, some kind of televangelist?"

"David, you don't have to be rude," Father Cliff said.

"I don't mind," Kenneth said, then said to David. "I'm a businessman—like you. I can show you my credentials."

David grunted. "Then tell me about this mysterious Foster Fund. Why did my dad give so much of his money to it—and for what purpose?"

Kenneth shoved his hands into his coat pocket. "You were probably just becoming a teenager when your father first approached me about the idea."

"*He* approached *you*?"

"That's right. He had received a windfall from various investments he'd made and wanted to establish a fund, something to help students with their college costs."

"You mean, scholarships?" Jonathan asked.

"That was part of it," Kenneth replied. "But, yes, he wanted to financially help hardworking students finish their education."

David stared at Kenneth.

"I suppose he was thinking about you three," Kenneth continued. "But, as was generally the case with your father, it made him think about others in need. So, he started the Foster Fund."

The meaning of it all was still lost to them. I could tell that Ruth and Jonathan didn't know what to make of it, nor did they understand why David had made such a fuss.

David was stone-faced as he looked out over the pond. "Is that it?"

Kenneth nodded. "That's the gist of it."

"Your father intended to put the three of you on the board but died before he made it official," Father Cliff said.

"A scholarship scheme," David said as if the concept was foreign to him.

"A lot of young people were given a chance they might not have had otherwise. I have a list of the recipients if you want to see them," Kenneth reached for his inside pocket and produced an envelope.

"Why would I care to see who benefited from my father's generosity when I didn't?" David said bitterly.

Ruth gasped. "David!"

"You didn't get anything from this Foster Fund, did you?" David said to her. He nodded to Jonathan. "What about you?"

"Your names are on this list," Kenneth said.

"What?" David nearly slipped on the ice. Jonathan reached out to steady him.

"You were one of the recipients. Those scholarships you received from the college to finish your education were drawn from the Foster Fund," Kenneth said.

He handed David the envelope.

David blinked, stunned, as if someone had slapped him hard across the face. He looked down at the envelope, then back at Kenneth.

"You benefited as well, Jonathan," Kenneth added.

Jonathan took a deep breath. "I wouldn't be a bit surprised."

David tore open the envelope and scanned the columns of names on the Foster Fund's official letterhead. His mouth fell open. His cheeks flushed.

His name was there in the middle of the list, along with the amount of money distributed to the Mendoza College of Business at Notre Dame for David's tuition.

After a moment of silence, Father Cliff cleared his throat and said: "He called it the Foster Fund because of his brother—your uncle."

"Brother?" Jonathan asked. "My dad doesn't have a brother."

"He did at one time."

Jonathan was dumbfounded. "Dad had a brother?"

"What happened to him?" Ruth asked, shocked.

"Your father was a twin," Father Cliff said. "His brother died at birth."

Now all three of them stood there with their mouths gaping.

"Just like Elvis," Jonathan said softly.

Kenneth said, "The Foster Fund was your father's pet project—a secret he and your mother kept because they didn't want undue credit. Our instructions were that no one should know until after he died. And even then, we were to only answer those people who specifically asked. You asked."

The truth was that I'd established the Foster Fund for David. I realized early on in his life that he was a stubborn, self-sufficient "I wanna do it myself" child. I thought he would only ever respect those things he could earn himself, so I outwardly provided the essentials he needed. In some ways, I gave him less than I provided Jonathan and Ruth in their lives.

As I began to think about how to help him with college, I decided that it would be a good idea to let him "earn" his way—through the kind of hard work that would earn a scholarship, a reward for his good grades. I wanted him to feel a sense of accomplishment. He could own his success without feeling he owed any of it to me.

I didn't realize that it had put a wedge between us all these years. He had obviously interpreted my secret help as some kind of abandonment. Now it grieved my heart.

"David," Kenneth said, as if he knew what I was thinking. "If you've been hurt by this news about the fund, I'm sorry. But I can promise you that your father's intentions were solid. He believed you were a determined, self-sufficient child and would only respect yourself if you worked hard for what was given to you. He wanted to help you in a way that didn't look like he was helping you. You received those funds because you earned them. Would you have wanted it any other way?"

David slowly shook his head.

Kenneth addressed all three of my children. "I'm going to miss your father terribly." He turned and walked back to the house.

"I'm sorry I couldn't tell you myself, David," Father Cliff said. "Your father's instructions were clear." He followed Kenneth.

David looked out at the pond. His face was screwed up as if he wanted to cry but refused to do it. "I feel like a first-class fool."

Jonathan chided him: "So you can't even travel economy as a fool. You have to be first class."

"I'm a fool either way."

"Why?" Jonathan asked. "Because of the Foster Fund? Nah. You're a fool for other reasons than that." Jonathan also turned and walked away.

David faced Ruth. "Any potshots you'd like to take while I'm down? Go on. You may never get this chance again."

Ruth said thoughtfully, "We didn't know him, did we? Not like we thought."

"No. I guess we didn't." David turned on his heels and walked off towards the other side of the pond.

Ted Hagan appeared on the path from the house. "Anyone want some coffee?" he asked.

I couldn't leave David. We sat together on a rock on the far side of the pond where he cried alone, just as he'd cried in the hotel bathroom. He leaned forward, elbows on his knees, and closed his eyes as if he were praying.

I had hoped to be vindicated by Kenneth Walsh's information about the Foster Fund. I was, in a way. But to what end? As I looked at my son, I tried to discern what he was thinking and feeling. This time I couldn't. Like Jonathan's shoulder getting in the way of my seeing his painting, something about David blocked my seeing, or getting impressions of, where his heart was. I supposed that he had a brand-new set of issues to deal with. What was he supposed to do with this anger he'd nurtured over the years? It wasn't going to magically disappear simply because he'd been corrected about his perceptions of me. If anything, he might feel betrayed because I'd kept such a large secret from him. Or perhaps he felt tricked. What was he going to do? Would his anger win out or would he allow for a measure of grace?

I should have talked to him long ago. I should have explained who I thought he was and how that had affected my actions towards him. I should have said that parents don't treat their children the same; they try to adjust to their children's personalities and do what's right for them as individuals. Perhaps if I'd spoken to him man-to-man earlier on, we could have had better father-to-son conversations later. But I didn't. I didn't know how he was truly feeling. *I didn't know*. As a parent, I'd always followed the basic rules I'd learned from *my* parents: love your children, discipline them as needed, and pray for them everyday.

But was that enough?

I look at the tangled emotions of my three children and suspected that it wasn't. But I was at a loss as to what more I could have done.

What more could I have done? There were no guarantees in parenting. No established formulas. No easy steps. *What more could I have done?*

I felt the full force of regret and wondered: *Is this why I'd been placed in an after-life holding tank, so I could see the consequences of my best intentions and worst judgements? Yes, I suppose it was. I know that Purgatory, in the Catholic sense, is a place of cleansing—a place where we are all given a good, thorough, and somewhat painful scrubbing before going in to the presence of our King. I hoped that was true. If not—if watching my children play out the consequences of my bad decisions and poor communication was what I was here to do—then I was in a terrible place that seemed more like Hell than anything else. Why torture me with what I could not change?*

"Forgive me, son," I heard myself saying.

He couldn't hear me, I knew. His eyes were still closed. His thoughts and feelings were blocked to me. If indeed he was praying, then he wasn't talking to me anyway.

He slowly stood up and walked in the opposite direction from the house.

I couldn't follow him.

Chapter Ten

THE WINTER light faded quickly. Too quickly, I thought, when I returned to the house. Something had changed. Time *felt* different, though I wasn't sure why.

The guests were gone. The house showed no signs of their presence. Ted Hagan stood in the living room wearing a nice suit and overcoat. When had he changed clothes?

"Are you coming?" he shouted out.

Ruth's voice came from somewhere upstairs. "Yes, give me just a minute!"

"Do you want to go with us?" Ruth asked Jonathan, who had dropped himself into my easy chair with a glass of spiked eggnog.

"No, thanks," Jonathan said. "I think I'll just sit here and listen to Elvis all night."

"Is that the best way to celebrate the Birth of Jesus?" Ted asked.

Jonathan shrugged. "When Elvis sang the gospel, he sang it with his soul. It's not exactly a church service, but it's as much as I want right now."

Ted frowned at him.

Jonathan smiled. "I'm planning to go to Mass in the morning," he said. "You don't really think I'd miss Mass on Christmas, do you?"

Ted looked as if he actually thought Jonathan might.

Midnight Mass? Had I leapt from the day of my funeral to Christmas Eve? I glanced at the tree. There were wrapped presents underneath.

Ruth came into the room wearing a festive dress of dark green and burgundy trim. Ted helped her into her coat. She then stepped over to Jonathan, knelt down, and kissed him on the cheek. "Please come with us," she said.

Jonathan shook his head. And I suddenly knew that he was thinking of his unfinished painting. "Tomorrow," he said.

Ruth gave Ted a signal to leave them alone for a moment. He nodded and went into the kitchen. A moment later they heard him tidying up some of the unwashed dishes, more loudly than usual. Ruth sat on the arm of my easy chair and took Jonathan's hand. "Are you all right?"

"I keep thinking about the news that Dad had a twin brother who'd died."

"Just like Elvis," she said.

"Just like Elvis." He took a sip of his eggnog.

"There's more," Ruth said. "What else are you thinking?"

He looked at her.

She said, "I see that knot you get between your eyes when you're thinking hard. There's something else on your mind."

Jonathan sat quietly for a moment, then said: "I was just thinking about how little we really know our parents. I mean, if David was so wrong about Dad, then maybe I'm wrong about some things, too."

"Like what?"

Jonathan hesitated, fixing his eyes on the lights of the tree. "I didn't become the painter that Dad wanted me to be. I failed him."

Ruth gave a slight groan as if a tiny bit of anguish had slipped out of her heart. "Where did you get that idea, Jonathan? Dad loved you. He was proud of your talent."

"Was he?" Jonathan asked. "Then why can't I escape this feeling that he was disappointed in me?"

"*Disappointed*—in *you*?" Ruth asked. "If he was disappointed in anybody, it was *me*."

Jonathan sat up, nearly spilling his drink. "Not a chance. He cherished you. You were his princess. Why would he be disappointed in you?"

Ruth took Jonathan's glass of eggnog and drank some of it. "I made some bad choices. I…did things that he wouldn't have been proud of. I'm…"

Jonathan observed her for a moment, then said quietly. "Which one of us hasn't? I don't think Dad imagined we were saints."

"But I was his *angel*." Her eyes washed over with tears, but she fought them away.

Jonathan shifted in the chair to face her. "Now, Ruth—"

She stood up. "I have to go."

Jonathan searched for the words, but they wouldn't come. They were kindred spirits with a kindred problem, and now they seemed unable to help each other through it.

Ted appeared in the doorway.

Ruth and Jonathan looked at him expectantly. So did I.

He said in a nervous voice, "I made as much noise as I could with those dishes, but I still caught part of what you were saying."

Ruth blushed and turned her face from him.

"I've spent a lot of time with your father over the past year or so. We talked about a lot of things. Sometimes we talked about you . . ." He swallowed hard. "I think you two have got it all wrong."

Jonathan looked at him skeptically. "How so?"

Ted sat down on the edge of the couch and twisted his dish towel around his hands. "This is out of line, I know. But I hate the way you guys keep torturing yourselves. I think you have to stop and ask yourselves a question."

"What question?"

"You have to ask: who's talking here?"

Ruth and Jonathan glanced at each other. "What do you mean?" Ruth asked.

"Is this your father talking—or your guilt?" Ted swallowed hard again. The dish towel was wrapped so tightly around his left hand that his fingers turned red. "What you're saying doesn't sound like your father at all. He never talked like he was disappointed with either of you. Ever."

"He wouldn't say it out loud," Jonathan said.

Ted shifted uneasily. "I know he didn't like it when you did stupid things or hurt yourselves, but he never said anything about failing him or letting him down. I honestly don't think such ideas occurred to him. He loved you and wanted you to be happy."

Silence hung over them like the scent of the Christmas tree.

Ted paused, as if choosing his next words carefully. "If he ever suffered any heartache, it was because he knew that you weren't happy with some of the decisions you'd made. And he didn't know how to help you fix them. Not without being intrusive, I mean. He hated the idea of being intrusive. I guess that's why he created the Foster Fund." Ted freed his strangled hand from the dish towel.

"So, instead of trying to fix your problems, he prayed for you. *We* prayed for you."

Ruth sighed deeply.

Jonathan shook his head sadly. "Well" was all he said.

"Don't drive yourselves crazy second-guessing what you don't know," Ted said as he stood up. "Paint or don't paint, Jonathan. But make your decision because of what *you* want, not because of something you imagine about your father's feelings." He reached a hand out to Ruth. "And as for you, young lady..."

Ruth watched him with an expression of obvious affection. She took his hand.

He smiled, red-faced. "If we don't get a move-on, we're going to be late for Mass."

Just as they reached the door, Jonathan said, "I don't care what David says about you, Ted, I think you're all right."

Ted didn't know whether it was a compliment or not. He nodded all the same.

"Where is David?" Ruth asked.

With that question I suddenly got an impression about David: he had made himself scarce, barely speaking to either Ruth or Jonathan since the pond and hadn't been around the house all of Christmas Eve.

"Maybe he took off like he did after Mom's funeral," Ruth said.

"If he ran off, then he wasn't very smart about it. His rental car is still outside, and his suitcase is in his room. He wouldn't leave them behind," Jonathan said, then added wryly, "Though, if he did, I've got dibs on the suitcase. It's worth a couple of hundred dollars."

Ruth laughed, dashed back to the easy chair, kissed him on the cheek, and then left with Ted.

Jonathan sat in the dim light of the living room, bathed in the green, red, blue, and yellow of the lights. The tinsel and ornaments helped create an ethereal, almost transcendent, experience. Elvis's voice worked through the atmosphere of the room.

The room had changed so little in the past thirty years that Jonathan felt as if he could be transported back through time to any point in his memories of Christmases past. He saw himself as a boy, receiving his first paint set. He thought of his earliest drawings of the life of Jesus—the very things that made him want to draw in the first place. The miracles, the Cross, the Resurrection...

Where had he gone wrong with his painting? he wondered. What had he lost along the way?

He mused on the revelations of the past couple of days: the Foster Fund, my dead twin, David's behavior—and his own realization that his perceptions of me needed adjusting.

One can paint a portrait of someone that is exact in its duplication of the details but may miss the essence of the person; the character, personality, or soul. He didn't say the words out loud, but I heard them as if he did. *Just as an artist can paint a portrait that seems to be lacking in its exact duplication of the details but captures the heart and soul of the person.*

Why? He wondered. *What accounts for the difference?*

It must be the inexplicable ability of the artist to connect to the very soul of his subject; an intuitive understanding of the person *behind* the artifice of skin, hair, facial features, and body.

Agitated, Jonathan pushed himself out of the chair and paced around the room. He wondered if I had ever sat for a portrait, could he have painted me? Technically, yes. But could he have painted the *real* me? He wasn't so sure that he could. He was no longer so certain he knew me at all.

Jonathan's mind whirled in several directions at once. Then he suddenly grabbed his coat and nearly raced out of the house. He walked with purpose, but I don't think he knew where he was going.

At first he went in the direction of the St. Clare's, and I thought he might attend Midnight Mass after all. But he strolled past it without stopping or even responding to the sounds of "O Come, All Ye Faithful" that came joyfully from inside, like a chorus of angels on shepherd's hills. He continued on to downtown Hope Springs. The offices and shops had now closed hours before. The decorations, strewn across the street from lamppost to lamppost, swayed gently, the cheap tinseled letters wishing a Merry Christmas to his eyes alone. He pressed on past through the town, then turned left on Sycamore and walked past the barren trees and the old high school to Church Road—and doubled-back to St. Clare's. He reached the iron fence bordering the cemetery, and then the large entry gate. It was closed and locked, but a small entry door to the right was open. He walked purposefully through the graveyard, weaving in and out of the tombstones, until he reached Kathryn's and my grave.

He stood there, breathless, as if we'd been waiting for him and he was late.

Kathryn Anne Lee her side of the tombstone said, *Beloved Wife and Mother*, and her birth- and death-days. *Richard Aaron Lee*, my side said, and the rest was unfinished. I had died too quickly and around a holiday so Tommy Edmonston at his family's masonry shop hadn't had a chance to fill in the remaining inscriptions.

"Just like Elvis," he said as he looked at my name. He'd known for years that Elvis and I shared the same middle name—through no contrivance of my parents, it was just a coincidence. From his expression I sensed a greater significance to it now.

Then his thoughts came like an explosion, spinning past and around me.

"What happened?" he asked out loud, as if to me. "Have I lost sight of the soul of my subject? The soul of my work?"

No sooner were those questions asked, then his mind went back to Elvis, and I saw a montage of images of the young swivel-hipped singer who had shocked the world with his voice and style, the leather-jacketed Elvis, the Hollywood Elvis, the Vegas Elvis, the bloated Elvis who'd become a mockery of his original self.

Where did he go wrong? Jonathan wondered. His roots, the essence of his art, were in the gospel music of his church. It had resonated in a raw faith and found its voice in his singing. But he had lost that somewhere along the way.

What happened? Did he stop hearing the music in his heart? Did he forget why he loved the music in the first place? How does an artist like Elvis get lost along the way?

Jonathan remembered reading somewhere how, later in life, Elvis regretted moving so far away from his gospel roots. Without the gospel, there was no blues. Without the blues, there was no rock-and-roll. It was said that in the days leading up to his death, he got out of bed only to sing gospel songs at his piano. It was also claimed that he was reading a book called *The Face of Jesus* when he died. Were these things symptoms of something stirring deeper within Elvis—the yearning that St. Augustine recognized, and every artist suffers as an integral part of the creative process.

Had Elvis recognized too late that he had lost sight of the very thing that energized his music: his *soul*?

Jonathan remembered again the feelings he had when, as a boy, he tried to draw the miracles of Jesus. What was lacking in his technical excellence was made up for by his passion for the miracles—his sense of wonder and awe of them. His earliest works were energized by his faith. But something changed. He had become a better artist technically, but... *something changed.*

A pale moon peeked through a clearing sky. Jonathan took a deep breath and exhaled, a cloud of his breath rising into the night. He had gone the way of Elvis without realizing it. Blaming his artistic block on my disappointment was a deception. His artistic block came from a deeper and more significant place. He saw it now. Like Elvis, he had lost touch with the very thing that made his creativity possible. His soul.

Suddenly Jonathan and I were standing together in the living room, looking on as his younger self, a boy of eight, brought home pictures he'd drawn at school. He'd sketched the story of Jesus healing a blind man. But the face of Jesus was blank.

I asked him then why he hadn't drawn it.

Jonathan looked puzzled. He frowned. "It's because *I* can't see Jesus's face. I... can't see it in my head," he replied sadly.

Then, like a film edit, we cut to: "Mrs. Ashley at school says I can't draw someone I don't really know. I need to *know* Jesus in my heart before I can draw his face."

Dear Mrs. Ashley. A true Baptist.

I said to him at the time: "Knowing him in your heart is very important, but not only so you can draw him. You need to know him for greater reasons than that."

A church bell rang in the steeple of All Saints Episcopal Church on the other side of town. I smiled. The electronic timer on that bell had been twenty-five minutes off for weeks.

The thoughts came to Jonathan afresh. *I can't paint a good portrait of someone I don't know. A person is more than lines and shadows.*

Ignoring the snow and slush, Jonathan knelt at the foot of my grave. The church bells rang again with what sounded to him like a low and solemn *now.*

My hands cannot paint what my heart doesn't know, Jonathan concluded.

It was Christmas Day, the birth of the babe in the manger, the Christ child. *More than lines and shadows.* The only way back to his soul was to *know* Christ, to see him anew.

Jonathan looked up at the sky and into the face of the pale moon. His eyes were misty. His lips trembled.

Heal my blindness, he whispered, *so I may see.*

Then he heard the words of another man from centuries ago. *I believe. Help me with my unbelief.*

In the face of the pale moon, he saw the face of a child.

Chapter Eleven

THE IMAGE *of Jonathan on his knees by my grave fades from my sight.*

I see Ruth kneeling at Mass, her head bowed and her hands clasped across her belly as if she wants to hold the life within her. She is weeping.

I see David standing somewhere I don't recognize. His expression is one of expectancy. I don't know why.

Something tells me my time is limited now. But I don't want to leave this place, wherever it may be. I don't want to leave my children. Not yet.

Please God, not yet.

I am whisked home again and there is no doubt—if I ever had a doubt—that I am not in control of what I've been seeing, hearing, or perceiving.

Ruth sat in the living room, anxiously awaiting her brothers. She'd fixed some fresh coffee, re-spiked the eggnog, and placed a few more gifts under the tree. The fire she'd made in the fireplace crackled, casting an orange-yellow glow over the room, overruling the colors of the Christmas lights.

So where was Jonathan now, I wondered. Where was David?

In spite of the evidence to the contrary, Ruth was convinced that David had left, just as he had when his mother had died. She suspected he would call at some point and ask her to ship his clothes to him. She would refuse, telling him to come and get his own clothes—knowing, of course, that she'd do it as long as Jonathan got to keep the suitcase

The front door banged open, and she nearly fell off of the couch.

"It's me," David said as he walked into view. His arms were laden with wrapped Christmas packages. He carefully knelt next to the tree and placed them alongside Ruth's gifts.

"What's all this?" Ruth asked.

"Santa Claus has come to town." He took off his coat.

Ruth was dumbfounded. "Where in the world have you been?"

"Denver. I knew the stores would be open later there. Is there anything hot to drink?"

"Coffee—and some apple cider and eggnog. You *walked* to Denver?"

"Funny enough, I got a ride with Oz Trent in his pickup truck."

"Oz Trent?" Ruth asked. "The guy who used to clean Dad's office?"

"So you know him," David said, impressed.

"Why did you go all the way to Denver with Oz Trent?"

"Because I left my car here. I was taking a walk and walked further than I expected. Oz came by. I gave him some money to drive me to Denver and back." David spoke as if the whole explanation was as normal as could be. "Did you know he still plays 8-track tapes in his pickup?"

Ruth shook her head. "No. Why would I know that?"

"No reason," he replied and walked into the kitchen.

Ruth gazed at the presents and followed David. "When you disappeared today, I thought for sure you'd run off."

David was in the kitchen now, pouring coffee into two mugs. He handed her one and then sipped from his own, cupping it in his hands. "This is perfect. Oz's pickup truck has a problem with the exhaust. It fills the cab. We had to drive with the windows down or risk asphyxiation."

Ruth saw for the first time how red-cheeked he was. His eyes were moist and alive. It was a startling contrast to the hard, cynical look he normally had.

"I wanted to run," he said, returning to her earlier statement. "I wanted to get back to my life and my work and put this whole nonsense behind me."

"Why didn't you?"

David shrugged. "I knew Jonathan would walk off with my suitcase upstairs."

Ruth grinned.

Holding the mug tightly, David looked down as if there was something about the mug that deserved his attention. "Everything I thought I knew was wrong."

She looked at him with an expression that said: *you're not the only one who feels that way.*

"I don't like being wrong," David said. He looked solemn, his eyes still locked on the mug. "This'll come as a surprise to you, but . . . I'm not very good with relationships."

Ruth smiled at him.

"They're too complicated," he said. "Give me a contract that spells everything out in terms I can understand. And if I don't like the terms, then I negotiate or, barring that, I walk away."

"Is that why you left so quickly after Mom died?"

He nodded.

"What about now?"

"It's time for a change," he said simply. "I want to stay here for Christmas and get things sorted out. Maybe we can try to—"

He stopped because Ruth had put her mug on the counter and was moving towards him.

"What?" he asked.

She hugged him.

"Hey! Watch out for my coffee," he said, trying to hold the mug away to keep from spilling it. He patted her lightly on the back.

Ruth let go of him and stepped away.

David tried to sound nonchalant, but his voice took on a different tone that betrayed his sadness. He slowly turned the mug around so Ruth could see the inscription on the side. *Best Dad Ever*, it said.

"Dad did the best he could with us," David said. "I know his intentions were good when he set up the Foster Fund. It was an unconventional idea. But what else could he do with me? I was stubborn and spoiled then. I'm stubborn and spoiled now."

Ruth smiled and reached out to hug him again.

He stepped away from her. "Don't get so physical."

"Sorry," she said, her eyes alight with affection.

He continued, "Maybe things would've been different if he and I had talked, if I'd let him know how I felt, rather than stuff my feelings away for so long."

"That's true for all of us," she said.

"Anyway," he said, dismissing their entire conversation with a wave of his hand. "That's all I have to say. I've reached my quota of soul-bearing for this season."

"Thank you for telling me," she said with mock formality.

I was struck by a feeling of relief by his admission. Relief—and release. And I felt proud of him. It took a lot for him to admit all he had. He put the core of his very self on the line.

"What about you?" he asked.

Ruth frowned. I knew she was debating whether or not to tell him about the baby. Instead she said, "I don't want you to sell the house."

"Then what are we going to do with it?"

"I want to live here."

An eyebrow went up. "So you want to return to small-town living?" he asked.

"I want to return to *something*. Something I lost when I left here." She patted her heart. "Something here."

"Ted?"

Ruth blushed.

"He's a nice guy," David said. "A lot better than anyone you'll find in Los Angeles."

"I know."

They heard the front door open. Both David and Ruth moved from the kitchen to the living room. Jonathan threw his coat on a hook and walked past Ruth and David as if he didn't see them.

He had reached the bottom of the stairs when Ruth called out to him.

"Not now," he said and ascended the stairs two at a time.

"But we have to talk," she shouted after him. "You can't go to bed now."

"I'm not going to bed," he shouted back at her.

Chapter Twelve

I DON'T see the finished painting. Nor do I see whether or not Ruth and Ted get married. Nor do I see my grandbaby. Nor how David's change of heart affects the rest of his life. The picture, for the most part, disappears from me.

The only image I see solidly is of another Midnight Mass. Father Cliff Montgomery celebrates, as usual. I see my three children sitting in the pew that was our usual spot when we attended together as a family. But it is like looking at them through white heat: the image swaying and changing so that my children are adults, then teenagers, then children, then adults again. Intermittently, Kathryn and I are with them, too. Young, then middle-aged, then old, then young again. Is it a visual trick or is time passing quickly before my eyes?

I remember something that happened shortly after I learned to use a computer. The confounded contraption glitched one day and all the various files and manuscripts I had stored there suddenly appeared in rapid succession on the screen. There was no order to the very fast images that came and went in front of my eyes, faster and faster until the machine overloaded and the screen went blank.

What I see now is nearly like that. I have no other way to explain it. The scenes spin past me as if they are not bound by time or chronology, and yet I comprehend them fully. It occurs to me that everything I've been seeing since I died has gone past in the blink of an eye. Time doesn't exist here. For all I know, it has been the tiniest fraction of a second since I was standing next to the pond and felt that itch in my chest.

The scenes stop and the last thing I see is a young couple sitting in a movie theatre watching Elvis Presley in *Blue Hawaii*.

Then even that is gone. My life as I know it has finished.

The future belongs to the living. I know beyond a shadow of doubt that I am in an eternal place. A holy place.

I hear a voice singing "Love Me Tender," but it is not Elvis. It is my beloved. She is at once glorious to behold, but as much herself as she ever was.

"It turned out all right," I say to her as naturally as if we had actually been sitting and watching an Elvis movie.

She smiles. In the warmth of her smile, I feel a sense of completion.

"Is that what I was supposed to see?" I ask. Because she got here ahead of me, I assume she knows.

She looks at me with an expression that asks, *Supposed to see?*

"Was I supposed to learn that, in spite of our best efforts as parents, things go wrong and maybe they'll go right again?"

What makes you think you were supposed to learn anything?

"Wasn't I?"

Maybe it's only a reminder of what you already knew.

I'm confused. "A reminder?"

Just one, before you go on to other reminders.

"Remind me of *what*?" I ask her. "What did I already know?"

She turns and we are both looking at David sitting on the rock by the pond.

I recall the scene and what I thought at that moment. "Forgiveness?"

Forgiveness. Understanding. Reconciliation. Everything you were praying for up until you died.

"I didn't expect death to be part of the answer to my prayers," I say.

I do not see her smile as much as I feel its radiance. She holds out her hand for me to take. *There's someone you must meet. This way.*

"Should I be afraid?" I take her hand.

Why be afraid? she asks as she draws me forward. *You've come home.*